Frank Richard Stockton

The Lady, or the Tiger?

And other stories

Frank Richard Stockton

The Lady, or the Tiger?
And other stories

ISBN/EAN: 9783744748124

Printed in Europe, USA, Canada, Australia, Japan

Cover: Foto ©Andreas Hilbeck / pixelio.de

More available books at **www.hansebooks.com**

THE LADY, OR THE TIGER?

AND

OTHER STORIES

BY

FRANK R. STOCKTON

Author's Edition

EDINBURGH

DAVID DOUGLAS, CASTLE STREET

1884

Frederic Ernest Allsopp.

CONTENTS.

THE LADY, OR THE TIGER?

THE LADY, OR THE TIGER?

IN the very olden time, there lived a semi-barbaric king, whose ideas, though somewhat polished and sharpened by the progressiveness of distant Latin neighbours, were still large, florid, and untrammelled, as became the half of him which was barbaric. He was a man of exuberant fancy, and, withal, of an authority so irresistible that, at his will, he turned his varied fancies into facts. He was greatly given to self-communing; and, when he and himself agreed upon anything, the thing was done. When every member of his domestic and political systems moved smoothly in its appointed course, his nature was bland and genial; but whenever there was a little hitch, and some of his orbs got out of their orbits, he was blander and more genial still, for nothing pleased him so much as to make the crooked straight, and crush down uneven places.

Among the borrowed notions by which his barbarism had become semified was that of the public arena, in which, by exhibitions of manly and beastly valour, the minds of his subjects were refined and cultured.

But even here the exuberant and barbaric fancy asserted itself. The arena of the king was built, not to give the people an opportunity of hearing the rhapsodies of dying gladiators, nor to enable them to view the inevitable conclusion of a conflict between religious opinions and hungry jaws, but for purposes far better adapted to widen and develop the mental energies of the people. This vast amphitheatre, with its encircling galleries, its mysterious vaults, and its unseen passages, was an agent of poetic justice, in which crime was punished, or virtue rewarded, by the decrees of an impartial and incorruptible chance.

When a subject was accused of a crime of sufficient importance to interest the king, public notice was given that on an appointed day the fate of the accused person would be decided in the king's arena,—a structure which well deserved its name ; for, although its form and plan were borrowed from afar, its purpose emanated solely from the brain of this man, who, every barleycorn a king, knew no tradition to which he owed more allegiance than pleased his fancy, and who ingrafted on every adopted form of human thought and action the rich growth of his barbaric idealism.

When all the people had assembled in the galleries, and the king, surrounded by his court, sat high up on his throne of royal state on one side of the arena, he gave a signal, a door beneath him opened, and the accused subject stepped out into the amphitheatre. Directly opposite him, on the other side of the enclosed space, were two doors, exactly alike and side by side. It was the duty and the privilege of the person on trial to walk directly to these doors and open one of them. He could open either door he pleased : he was subject to no guidance or influence but that of the aforementioned impartial and incorruptible chance. If he opened the one, there came out of it a hungry tiger, the fiercest and most cruel that could be procured, which immediately sprang upon him, and tore him to pieces, as a punishment for his guilt. The moment that the case of the criminal was thus decided, doleful iron bells were clanged, great wails went up from the hired mourners posted on the outer rim of the arena, and the vast audience, with bowed heads and downcast hearts, wended slowly their homeward way, mourning greatly that one so young and fair, or so old and respected, should have merited so dire a fate.

But, if the accused person opened the other door, there came forth from it a lady, the most suitable to his years and station that his majesty could select among his fair subjects ; and to this lady he was immediately married, as a reward of his innocence. It mattered not that he might already possess a wife and family, or that his affections might be engaged upon an object of his own selection : the king allowed no such subordinate arrangements to interfere with his great scheme of retribution and reward. The exercises, as in the other instance, took place immediately, and in the arena. Another door opened beneath the king, and a priest, followed by a band of choristers, and dancing maidens blowing joyous airs on golden horns and treading an epithalamic measure, advanced to where the pair stood, side by side ; and the wedding was promptly and cheerily solemnised. Then the gay brass bells rang forth their merry peals, the people shouted glad hurrahs, and the innocent man, preceded by children strewing flowers on his path, led his bride to his home.

This was the king's semi-barbaric method of administering justice. Its perfect fairness is obvious. The criminal could not know out of which door would come the lady: he opened either he pleased, without having the slightest idea whether, in the next instant, he was to be devoured or married. On some occasions the tiger came out of one door, and on some out of the other. The decisions of this tribunal were not only fair, they were positively determinate: the accused person was instantly punished if he found himself guilty; and, if innocent, he was rewarded on the spot, whether he liked it or not. There was no escape from the judgments of the king's arena.

The institution was a very popular one. When the people gathered together on one of the great trial days, they never knew whether they were to witness a bloody slaughter or a hilarious wedding. This element of uncertainty lent an interest to the occasion which it could not otherwise have attained. Thus, the masses were entertained and pleased, and the thinking part of the community could bring no charge of unfairness against this plan; for did not the accused person have the whole matter in his own hands?

This semi-barbaric king had a daughter as blooming as his most florid fancies, and with a soul as fervent and imperious as his own. As is usual in such cases, she was the apple of his eye, and was loved by him above all humanity. Among his courtiers was a young man of that fineness of blood and lowness of station common to the conventional heroes of romance who love royal maidens. This royal maiden was well satisfied with her lover, for he was handsome and brave to a degree unsurpassed in all this kingdom; and she loved him with an ardour that had enough of barbarism in it to make it exceedingly warm and strong. This love affair moved on happily for many months, until one day the king happened to discover its existence. He did not hesitate nor waver in regard to his duty in the premises. The youth was immediately cast into prison, and a day was appointed for his trial in the king's arena. This, of course, was an especially important occasion; and his majesty, as well as all the people, was greatly interested in the workings and development of this trial. Never before had such a case occurred; never before had a subject dared to love the daughter of a king. In after-years such things became commonplace enough; but then they were, in no slight degree, novel and startling.

The tiger-cages of the kingdom were searched for the most savage and relentless beasts, from which the fiercest monster might be selected for the arena; and the ranks of maiden youth and beauty throughout the land were carefully surveyed by competent judges, in order that the young man might have a fitting bride in case fate did not determine for him a different destiny. Of course, everybody knew that the deed with which the accused was charged had been done. He had loved the princess, and neither he, she, nor any one else thought of denying the fact; but the king would not think of allowing any fact of this kind to interfere with the workings of the tribunal, in which he took such great delight and satisfaction. No matter how the affair turned out, the youth would be disposed of; and the king would take an æsthetic pleasure in watching the course of events, which would determine whether or not the young man had done wrong in allowing himself to love the princess.

The appointed day arrived. From far and near the people gathered, and thronged the great galleries of the arena; and crowds,

unable to gain admittance, massed themselves against its outside walls. The king
and his court were in their places, opposite
the twin doors,—those fateful portals, so
terrible in their similarity.

All was ready. The signal was given. A
door beneath the royal party opened, and
the lover of the princess walked into the
arena. Tall, beautiful, fair, his appearance
was greeted with a low hum of admiration
and anxiety. Half the audience had not
known so grand a youth had lived among
them. No wonder the princess loved him !
What a terrible thing for him to be there !

As the youth advanced into the arena, he
turned, as the custom was, to bow to the
king : but he did not think at all of that
royal personage ; his eyes were fixed upon
the princess, who sat to the right of her
father. Had it not been for the moiety of
barbarism in her nature, it is probable that
lady would not have been there ; but her
intense and fervid soul would not allow her
to be absent on an occasion in which she
was so terribly interested. From the
moment that the decree had gone forth,
that her lover should decide his fate in the
king's arena, she had thought of nothing,
night or day, but this great event and the

various subjects connected with it. Possessed of more power, influence, and force of character than any one who had ever before been interested in such a case, she had done what no other person had done,—she had possessed herself of the secret of the doors. She knew in which of the two rooms, that lay behind those doors, stood the cage of the tiger, with its open front, and in which waited the lady. Through these thick doors, heavily curtained with skins on the inside, it was impossible that any noise or suggestion should come from within to the person who should approach to raise the latch of one of them ; but gold, and the power of a woman's will, had brought the secret to the princess.

And not only did she know in which room stood the lady ready to emerge, all blushing and radiant, should her door be opened, but she knew who the lady was. It was one of the fairest and loveliest of the damsels of the court who had been selected as the reward of the accused youth, should he be proved innocent of the crime of aspiring to one so far above him ; and the princess hated her. Often had she seen, or imagined that she had seen, this fair creature throwing glances of admiration upon the person of her lover, and sometimes she thought these glances were perceived and even returned. Now and then she had seen them talking together; it was but for a moment or two, but much can be said in a brief space; it may have been on most unimportant topics, but how could she know that? The girl was lovely, but she had dared to raise her eyes to the loved one of the princess; and, with all the intensity of the savage blood transmitted to her through long lines of wholly barbaric ancestors, she hated the woman who blushed and trembled behind that silent door.

When her lover turned and looked at her, and his eye met hers as she sat there paler and whiter than any one in the vast ocean of anxious faces about her, he saw, by that power of quick perception which is given to those whose souls are one, that she knew behind which door crouched the tiger, and behind which stood the lady. He had expected her to know it. He understood her nature, and his soul was assured that she would never rest until she had made plain to herself this thing, hidden to all other lookers-on, even to the king. The only hope for the youth in which there was any element of certainty was based upon the success of the princess in discovering this mystery; and the moment he looked upon her, he saw she had succeeded, as in his soul he knew she would succeed.

Then it was that his quick and anxious glance asked the question: "Which?" It was as plain to her as if he shouted it from where he stood. There was not an instant to be lost. The question was asked in a flash; it must be answered in another.

Her right arm lay on the cushioned parapet before her. She raised her hand, and made a slight, quick movement toward the right. No one but her lover saw her. Every eye but his was fixed on the man in the arena.

He turned, and with a firm and rapid step he walked across the empty space. Every heart stopped beating, every breath was held, every eye was fixed immoveably upon that man. Without the slightest hesitation, he went to the door on the right, and opened it.

Now, the point of the story is this: Did the tiger come out of that door, or did the lady?

The more we reflect upon this question, the harder it is to answer. It involves a study of the human heart which leads us through devious mazes of passion, out of which it is difficult to find our way. Think of it, fair reader, not as if the decision of the question depended upon yourself, but upon that hot-blooded, semi-barbaric princess, her soul at a white heat beneath the combined fires of despair and jealousy. She had lost him, but who should have him?

How often, in her waking hours and in her dreams, had she started in wild horror, and covered her face with her hands as she thought of her lover opening the door on the other side of which waited the cruel fangs of the tiger!

But how much oftener had she seen him at the other door! How in her grievous reveries had she gnashed her teeth, and torn her hair, when she saw his start of rapturous delight as he opened the door of the lady! How her soul had burned in agony when she had seen him rush to meet that woman, with her flushing cheek and sparkling eye of triumph; when she had seen him lead her forth, his whole frame kindled with the joy of recovered life; when she had heard the glad shouts from the multitude, and the wild ringing of the happy bells; when she had seen the priest, with

his joyous followers, advance to the couple,
and make them man and wife before her
very eyes ; and when she had seen them
walk away together upon their path of
flowers, followed by the tremendous shouts
of the hilarious multitude, in which her one
despairing shriek was lost and drowned !

Would it not be better for him to die at
once, and go to wait for her in the blessed
regions of semi-barbaric futurity ?

And yet, that awful tiger, those shrieks,
that blood !

Her decision had been indicated in an
instant, but it had been made after days and
nights of anguished deliberation. She had
known she would be asked, she had decided
what she would answer, and, without the
slightest hesitation, she had moved her hand
to the right.

The question of her decision is one not to
be lightly considered, and it is not for me to
presume to set myself up as the one person
able to answer it. And so I leave it with all
of you : Which came out of the opened door,
—the lady, or the tiger?

THE TRANSFERRED GHOST.

THE TRANSFERRED GHOST.

THE country residence of Mr. John Hinckman was a delightful place to me, for many reasons. It was the abode of a genial, though somewhat impulsive, hospitality. It had broad, smooth-shaven lawns and towering oaks and elms; there were bosky shades at several points, and not far from the house there was a little rill spanned by a rustic bridge with the bark on; there were fruits and flowers, pleasant people, chess, billiards, rides, walks, and fishing. These were great attractions; but none of them, nor all of them together, would have been sufficient to hold me to the place very long. I had been invited for the trout season, but should, probably, have finished my visit early in the summer had it not been that upon fair days, when the grass was dry, and the sun was not too hot, and there was but little wind, there strolled beneath the lofty elms, or passed lightly through the bosky shades, the form of my Madeline.

This lady was not, in very truth, my Madeline. She had never given herself to me, nor had I, in any way, acquired possession of her. But as I considered her possession the only sufficient reason for the continuance of my existence, I called her, in my reveries, mine. It may have been that I would not have been obliged to confine the use of this possessive pronoun to my reveries had I confessed the state of my feelings to the lady.

But this was an unusually difficult thing to do. Not only did I dread, as almost all lovers dread, taking the step which would in an instant put an end to that delightful season which may be termed the ante-interrogatory period of love, and which might at the same time terminate all intercourse or connection with the object of my passion; but I was, also, dreadfully afraid of John Hinckman. This gentleman was a good friend of mine, but it would have required a bolder man than I was at that time to ask him for the gift of his niece, who was the head of his household, and, according to his own frequent statement, the main prop of his declining years. Had Madeline acquiesced in my general views on the subject, I might have felt encouraged to open the matter to Mr. Hinckman; but, as I said before, I had never asked her whether or not she would be mine. I thought of these things at all hours of the day and night, particularly the latter.

I was lying awake one night, in the great bed in my spacious chamber, when, by the dim light of the new moon, which partially filled the room, I saw John Hinckman standing by a large chair near the door. I was very much surprised at this for two reasons. In the first place, my host had never before come into my room; and, in the second place, he had gone from home that morning, and had not expected to return for several days. It was for this reason that I had been able that evening to sit much later than usual with Madeline on the moonlit porch. The figure was certainly that of John Hinckman in his ordinary dress, but there was a vagueness and indistinctness about it which presently assured me that it was a ghost. Had the good old man been murdered? and had his spirit come to tell me of the deed, and to confide to me the protection of his dear —— ? My heart fluttered at what I was about to think, but at this instant the figure spoke.

"Do you know," he said, with a countenance that indicated anxiety, "if Mr. Hinck-man will return to-night?"

I thought it well to maintain a calm exterior, and I answered—

"We do not expect him."

"I am glad of that," said he, sinking into the chair by which he stood. "During the two years and a half that I have inhabited this house, that man has never before been away for a single night. You can't imagine the relief it gives me."

And as he spoke he stretched out his legs, and leaned back in the chair. His form became less vague, and the colours of his garments more distinct and evident, while an expression of gratified relief succeeded to the anxiety of his countenance.

"Two years and a half!" I exclaimed. "I don't understand you."

"It is fully that length of time," said the ghost, "since I first came here. Mine is not an ordinary case. But before I say anything more about it, let me ask you again if you are sure Mr. Hinckman will not return to-night."

"I am as sure of it as I can be of anything," I answered. "He left to-day for Bristol, two hundred miles away."

"Then I will go on," said the ghost, "for

I am glad to have the opportunity of talking to some one who will listen to me ; but if John Hinckman should come in and catch me here, I should be frightened out of my wits."

"This is all very strange," I said, greatly puzzled by what I had heard. "Are you the ghost of Mr. Hinckman ?"

This was a bold question, but my mind was so full of other emotions that there seemed to be no room for that of fear.

"Yes, I am his ghost," my companion replied, "and yet I have no right to be. And this is what makes me so uneasy, and so much afraid of him. It is a strange story, and, I truly believe, without precedent. Two years and a half ago John Hinckman was dangerously ill in this very room. At one time he was so far gone that he was really believed to be dead. It was in consequence of too precipitate a report in regard to this matter that I was, at that time, appointed to be his ghost. Imagine my surprise and horror, sir, when, after I had accepted the position and assumed its responsibilities, that old man revived, became convalescent, and eventually regained his usual health. My situation was now one of extreme delicacy and embarrassment. I had no power to return to my

original unembodiment, and I had no right
to be the ghost of a man who was not dead.
I was advised by my friends to quietly maintain my position, and was assured that, as
John Hinckman was an elderly man, it could
not be long before I could rightfully assume
the position for which I had been selected.
But I tell you, sir," he continued, with
animation, "the old fellow seems as vigorous
as ever, and I have no idea how much longer
this annoying state of things will continue.
I spend my time trying to get out of that
old man's way.   I must not leave this house,
and he seems to follow me everywhere.   I
tell you, sir, he haunts me."

"That is truly a queer state of things," I
remarked.   "But why are you afraid of him?
He couldn't hurt you."

"Of course he couldn't," said the ghost.
"But his very presence is a shock and terror
to me.   Imagine, sir, how you would feel if
my case were yours."

I could not imagine such a thing at all.
I simply shuddered.

"And if one must be a wrongful ghost at
all," the apparition continued, "it would be
much pleasanter to be the ghost of some man
other than John Hinckman.   There is in
him an irascibility of temper, accompanied

by a facility of invective, which is seldom
met with. And what would happen if he
were to see me, and find out, as I am sure he
would, how long and why I had inhabited his
house, I can scarcely conceive. I have seen
him in his bursts of passion ; and, although
he did not hurt the people he stormed at any
more than he would hurt me, they seemed to
shrink before him."

All this I knew to be very true. Had it
not been for this peculiarity of Mr. Hinckman, I might have been more willing to talk
to him about his niece.

"I feel sorry for you," I said, for I really
began to have a sympathetic feeling toward
this unfortunate apparition. "Your case is
indeed a hard one. It reminds me of those
persons who have had doubles, and I suppose
a man would often be very angry indeed
when he found that there was another being
who was personating himself."

"Oh ! the cases are not similar at all,"
said the ghost. "A double or doppelganger
lives on the earth with a man ; and, being
exactly like him, he makes all sorts of
trouble, of course. It is very different
with me. I am not here to live with Mr.
Hinckman. I am here to take his place.
Now, it would make John Hinckman very

angry if he knew that.   Don't you know it would?"

I assented promptly.

"Now that he is away I can be easy for a little while," continued the ghost; "and I am so glad to have an opportunity of talking to you. I have frequently come into your room, and watched you while you slept, but did not dare to speak to you for fear that if you talked with me Mr. Hinckman would hear you, and come into the room to know why you were talking to yourself."

"But would he not hear you?" I asked.

"Oh no!" said the other: "there are times when any one may see me, but no one hears me except the person to whom I address myself."

"But why did you wish to speak to me?" I asked.

"Because," replied the ghost, "I like occasionally to talk to people, and especially to some one like yourself, whose mind is so troubled and perturbed that you are not likely to be frightened by a visit from one of us. But I particularly wanted to ask you to do me a favour. There is every probability, so far as I can see, that John Hinckman will live a long time, and my situation is becoming insupportable. My great object at present is to get myself transferred, and I think that you may, perhaps, be of use to me."

"Transferred!" I exclaimed. "What do you mean by that?"

"What I mean," said the other, "is this: Now that I have started on my career, I have got to be the ghost of somebody, and I want to be the ghost of a man who is really dead."

"I should think that would be easy enough," I said. "Opportunities must continually occur."

"Not at all! not at all!" said my companion quickly. "You have no idea what a rush and pressure there is for situations of this kind. Whenever a vacancy occurs, if I may express myself in that way, there are crowds of applications for the ghost-ship."

"I had no idea that such a state of things existed," I said, becoming quite interested in the matter. "There ought to be some regular system, or order of precedence, by which you could all take your turns, like customers in a barber's shop."

"Oh dear, that would never do at all!" said the other. "Some of us would have to wait for ever. There is always a great rush whenever a good ghostship offers itself—while, as you know, there are some positions that no ohe would care for. And it was in consequence of my being in too great a hurry on an occasion of the kind that I got myself into my present disagreeable predicament, and I have thought that it might be possible that you would help me out of it. You might know of a case where an opportunity for a ghostship was not generally expected, but which might present itself at any moment. If you would give me a short notice, I know I could arrange for a transfer."

"What do you mean?" I exclaimed. "Do you want me to commit suicide? Or to undertake a murder for your benefit?"

"Oh, no, no, no!" said the other, with a vapoury smile. "I mean nothing of that kind. To be sure, there are lovers who are watched with considerable interest, such persons having been known, in moments of depression, to offer very desirable ghostships; but I did not think of anything of that kind in connection with you. You were the only person I cared to speak to, and I hoped that you might give me some information that would be of use; and, in return, I shall be very glad to help you in your love affair."

"You seem to know that I have such an affair," I said.

"Oh yes!" replied the other, with a little yawn. "I could not be here so much as I have been without knowing all about that."

There was something horrible in the idea of Madeline and myself having been watched by a ghost, even, perhaps, when we wandered together in the most delightful and bosky places. But then, this was. quite an exceptional ghost, and I could not have the objections to him which would ordinarily arise in regard to beings of his class.

"I must go now," said the ghost, rising; "but I will see you somewhere to-morrow night. And remember—you help me, and I'll help you."

I had doubts the next morning as to the propriety of telling Madeline anything about this interview, and soon convinced myself that I must keep silent on the subject. If she knew there was a ghost about the house, she would probably leave the place instantly. I did not mention the matter, and so regulated my demeanour that I am quite sure Madeline never suspected what had taken place. For some time I had wished that Mr. Hinckman would absent himself, for a day at least, from the premises. In such case I thought I might more easily nerve myself up to the point of speaking to Madeline on the subject of our future collateral existence ; and, now that the opportunity for such speech had really occurred, I did not feel ready to avail myself of it. What would become of me if she refused me ?

I had an idea, however, that the lady thought that, if I were going to speak at all, this was the time. She must have known that certain sentiments were afloat within me, and she was not unreasonable in her wish to see the matter settled one way or the other. But I did not feel like taking a bold step in the dark. If she wished me to ask her to give herself to me, she ought to offer me some reason to suppose that she would make the gift. If I saw no probability of such generosity, I would prefer that things should remain as they were.

That evening I was sitting with Madeline in the moonlit porch. It was nearly ten o'clock, and ever since supper-time I had been working myself up to the point of making an avowal of my sentiments. I had not positively determined to do this, but wished gradually to reach the proper point, when, if the prospect looked bright, I might speak. My companion appeared to understand the situation—at least, I imagined that the nearer I came to a proposal the more she seemed to expect it. It was certainly a very critical and important epoch in my life. If I spoke, I should make myself happy or miserable for ever ; and if I did not speak I had every reason to believe that the lady would not give me another chance to do so.

Sitting thus with Madeline, talking a little, and thinking very hard over these momentous matters, I looked up and saw the ghost, not a dozen feet away from us. He was sitting on the railing of the porch, one leg thrown up before him, the other dangling down as he leaned against a post. He was behind Madeline, but almost in front of me, as I sat facing the lady. It was fortunate that Madeline was looking out over the landscape, for I must have appeared very much startled. The ghost had told me that he would see me some time this night, but I did not think he would make his appearance when I was in the company of Madeline. If she should see the spirit of her uncle, I could not answer for the consequences. I made no exclamation, but the ghost evidently saw that I was troubled.

"Don't be afraid," he said, "I shall not let her see me; and she cannot hear me speak unless I address myself to her, which I do not intend to do."

I suppose I looked grateful.

"So you need not trouble yourself about that," the ghost continued; "but it seems to me that you are not getting along very well with your affair. If I were you, I should speak out without waiting any longer. You will never have a better chance. You are not likely to be interrupted; and, so far as I can judge, the lady seems disposed to listen to you favourably; that is, if she ever intends to do so. There is no knowing when John Hinckman will go away again; certainly not this summer. If I were in your place, I should never dare to make love to Hinckman's niece if he were anywhere about the place. If he should catch any one offering himself to Miss Madeline, he would then be a terrible man to encounter."

I agreed perfectly to all this.

"I cannot bear to think of him!" I ejaculated aloud.

"Think of whom?" asked Madeline, turning quickly toward me.

Here was an awkward situation. The long
speech of the ghost, to which Madeline paid
no attention, but which I heard with perfect
distinctness, had made me forget myself.

· It was necessary to explain quickly. Of
course, it would not do to admit that it was
of her dear uncle that I was speaking; and
so I mentioned hastily the first name I
thought of.

"Mr. Vilars," I said.

This statement was entirely correct; for I
never could bear to think of Mr. Vilars, who
was a gentleman who had, at various times,
paid much attention to Madeline.

"It is wrong for you to speak in that way
of Mr. Vilars," she said. "He is a remark-
ably well educated and sensible young man,
and has very pleasant manners. He expects
to be elected to the legislature this fall, and
I should not be surprised if he made his
mark. He will do well in a legislative body,
for whenever Mr. Vilars has anything to
say he knows just how and when to say it."

This was spoken very quietly, and without
any show of resentment, which was all very
natural, for if Madeline thought at all
favourably of me she could not feel dis-
pleased that I should have disagreeable
emotions in regard to a possible rival. The

concluding words contained a hint which I was not slow to understand. I felt very sure that if Mr. Vilars were in my present position he would speak quickly enough.

"I know it is wrong to have such ideas about a person," I said, "but I cannot help it."

The lady did not chide me, and after this she seemed even in a softer mood. As for me, I felt considerably annoyed, for I had not wished to admit that any thought of Mr. Vilars had ever occupied my mind.

"You should not speak aloud that way," said the ghost, "or you may get yourself into trouble. I want to see everything go well with you, because then you may be disposed to help me, especially if I should chance to be of any assistance to you, which I hope I shall be."

I longed to tell him that there was no way in which he could help me so much as by taking his instant departure. To make love to a young lady with a ghost sitting on the railing near by, and that ghost the apparition of a much-dreaded uncle, the very idea of whom in such a position and at such a time made me tremble, was a difficult, if not an impossible, thing to do; but I forbore to speak, although I may have looked my mind.

"I suppose," continued the ghost, "that you have not heard anything that might be of advantage to me. Of course, I am very anxious to hear; but if you have anything to tell me, I can wait until you are alone. I will come to you to-night in your room, or I will stay here until the lady goes away."

"You need not wait here," I said; "I have nothing at all to say to you."

Madeline sprang to her feet, her face flushed and her eyes ablaze.

"Wait here!" she cried. "What do you suppose I am waiting for? Nothing to say to me indeed!—I should think so! What should you have to say to me?"

. "Madeline," I exclaimed, stepping toward her, "let me explain."

But she had gone.

Here was the end of the world for me! I turned fiercely to the ghost.

"Wretched existence!" I cried. "You have ruined everything. You have blackened my whole life. Had it not been for you"—

But here my voice faltered. I could say no more.

"You wrong me," said the ghost. "I have not injured you. I have tried only to encourage and assist you, and it is your own folly that has done this mischief. But do not despair. Such mistakes as these can be explained. Keep up a brave heart. Good-bye."

And he vanished from the railing like a bursting soap-bubble.

I went gloomily to bed, but I saw no apparitions that night except those of despair and misery which my wretched thoughts called up. The words I had uttered had sounded to Madeline like the basest insult. Of course, there was only one interpretation she could put upon them.

As to explaining my ejaculations, that was impossible. I thought the matter over and over again as I lay awake that night, and I determined that I would never tell Madeline the facts of the case. It would be better for me to suffer all my life than for her to know that the ghost of her uncle haunted the house. Mr. Hinckman was away, and if she knew of his ghost she could not be made to believe that he was not dead. She might not survive the shock ! No, my heart could bleed, but I would never tell her.

The next day was fine, neither too cool nor too warm ; the breezes were gentle, and nature smiled. But there were no walks or rides with Madeline. She seemed to be much engaged during the day, and I saw but little of her. When we met at meals she was polite, but very quiet and reserved. She had evidently determined on a course of conduct, and had resolved to assume that, although I had been very rude to her, she did not understand the import of my words. It would be quite proper, of course, for her not to know what I meant by my expressions of the night before.

I was downcast and wretched, and said but little, and the only bright streak across the black horizon of my woe was the fact that she did not appear to be happy, although she affected an air of unconcern. The moonlit porch was deserted that evening, but wandering about the house I found Madeline in the library alone. She was reading, but I went in and sat down near her. I felt that, although I could not do so fully, I must in a measure explain my conduct of the night before. She listened quietly to a somewhat laboured apology I made for the words I had used.

"I have not the slightest idea what you meant," she said, "but you were very rude."

I earnestly disclaimed any intention of rudeness, and assured her, with a warmth of speech that must have made some impression upon her, that rudeness to her would be an action impossible to me. I said a great deal upon the subject, and implored her to believe that if it were not for a certain obstacle I could speak to her so plainly that she would understand everything.

She was silent for a time, and then she said, rather more kindly, I thought, than she had spoken before—

"Is that obstacle in any way connected with my uncle?"

"Yes," I answered, after a little hesitation, "it is, in a measure, connected with him."

She made no answer to this, and sat looking at her book, but not reading. From the expression of her face, I thought she was somewhat softened toward me. She knew her uncle as well as I did, and she may have been thinking that, if he were the obstacle that prevented my speaking (and there were many ways in which he might be that obstacle), my position would be such a hard one that it would excuse some wildness of speech and eccentricity of manner. I saw, too, that the warmth of my partial explanations had had some effect on her, and I began to believe that it might be a good thing for me to speak my mind without delay. No matter how she should receive my proposition, my relations with her could not be worse than they had been the previous night and day, and there was something in her face which encouraged me to hope that she might forget my foolish exclamations of the evening before if I began to tell her my tale of love.

I drew my chair a little nearer to her, and as I did so the ghost burst into the room from the doorway behind her. I say burst, although no door flew open and he made no noise. He was wildly excited, and waved his arms above his head. The moment I saw him my heart fell within me. With the entrance of that impertinent apparition every hope fled from me. I could not speak while he was in the room.

I must have turned pale; and I gazed steadfastly at the ghost, almost without seeing Madeline, who sat between us.

"Do you know," he cried, "that John Hinckman is coming up the hill? He will be here in fifteen minutes; and if you are doing anything in the way of love-making, you had better hurry it up. But this is not what I came to tell you. I have glorious news! At last I am transferred! Not forty minutes ago a Russian nobleman was murdered by the Nihilists. Nobody ever thought of him in connection with an immediate ghostship. My friends instantly applied for the situation for me, and obtained my transfer. I am off before that horrid Hinckman comes up the hill. The moment I reach my new position, I shall put off this hated semblance. Good-bye. You can't imagine how glad I am to be, at last, the real ghost of somebody."

"Oh!" I cried, rising to my feet, and stretching out my arms in utter wretchedness, "I would to Heaven you were mine!"

"I *am* yours," said Madeline, raising to me her tearful eyes.

THE SPECTRAL MORTGAGE.

THE SPECTRAL MORTGAGE.

TOWARD the close of a beautiful afternoon in early summer I stood on the
piazza of the spacious country-house which
was my home. I had just dined, and I
gazed with a peculiar comfort and delight
upon the wide - spreading lawn and the
orchards and groves beyond; and then,
walking to the other end of the piazza, I
looked out toward the broad pastures, from
which a fine drove of cattle were leisurely
coming home to be milked, and toward the
fields of grain, whose green was beginning
already to be touched with yellow. In-
voluntarily (for, on principle, I was opposed
to such feelings) a pleasant sense of possession came over me. It could not be long
before all this would virtually be mine.

About two years before, I had married
the niece of John Hinckman, the owner of
this fine estate. He was very old, and could
not be expected to survive much longer, and
had willed the property, without reserve, to

my wife. This, in brief, was the cause of my present sense of prospective possession; and although, as I said, I was principled against the voluntary encouragement of such a sentiment, I could not blame myself if the feeling occasionally arose within me. I had not married my wife for her uncle's money. Indeed, we had both expected that the marriage would result in her being entirely disinherited. His niece was John Hinckman's housekeeper and sole prop and comfort, and if she left him for me she expected no kindness at his hands. But she had not left him. To our surprise, her uncle invited us to live with him, and our relations with him became more and more amicable and pleasant, and Mr. Hinckman had, of late, frequently expressed to me his great satisfaction that I had proved to be a man after his own heart; that I took an interest in flocks and herds and crops; that I showed a talent for such pursuits; and that I would continue to give, when he was gone, the same care and attention to the place which it had been so long his greatest pleasure to bestow. He was old and ill now, and tired of it all; and the fact that I had not proved to be, as he had formerly supposed me, a mere city gentleman, was a great comfort to his declining days. We were deeply grieved to think that the old man must soon die. We would gladly have kept him with us for years; but, if he must go, it was pleasant to know that he and ourselves were so well satisfied with the arrangements that had been made. Think me not cold and heartless, high-minded reader. For a few moments put yourself in my place.

But had you, at that time, put yourself in my place on that pleasant piazza, I do not believe you would have cared to stay there long; for, as I stood gazing over the fields, I felt a touch upon my shoulder. I cannot say that I was actually touched, but I experienced a feeling which indicated that the individual who had apparently touched me would have done so had he been able. I instantly turned, and saw, standing beside me, a tall figure in the uniform of a Russian officer. I started back, but made no sound. I knew what the figure was. It was a spectre—a veritable ghost.

Some years before this place had been haunted. I knew this well, for I had seen the ghost myself. But before my marriage the spectre had disappeared, and had not been seen since; and I must admit that my satisfaction, when thinking of this estate, without mortgage or encumbrance, was much increased by the thought that even the ghost, who used to haunt the house, had now departed.

But here he was again. Although in different form and guise, I knew him. It was the same ghost.

" Do you remember me ? " said the figure.

" Yes," I answered : " I remember you in the form in which you appeared to me some time ago. Although your aspect is entirely changed, I feel you to be the same ghost that I have met before."

" You are right," said the spectre. " I am glad to see you looking so well, and apparently happy. But John Hinckman, I understand, is in a very low state of health."

" Yes," I said : " he is very old and ill. But I hope," I continued, as a cloud of anxiety began to rise within me, " that his expected decease has no connection with any prospects or plans of your own."

" No," said the ghost. " I am perfectly satisfied with my present position. I am off duty during the day ; and the difference in time between this country and Russia gives me opportunities of being here in your early evening, and of visiting scenes and localities which are very familiar and agreeable to me."

"Which fact, perhaps, you had counted upon when you first put this uniform on," I remarked.

The ghost smiled.

"I must admit, however," he said, "that I am seeking this position for a friend of mine, and I have reason to believe that he will obtain it."

"Good heavens!" I exclaimed. "Is it possible that this house is to be haunted by a ghost as soon as the old gentleman expires? Why should this family be tormented in such a horrible way? Everybody who dies does not have a ghost walking about his house."

"Oh no!" said the spectre. "There are thousands of positions of the kind which are never applied for; but the ghostship here is a very desirable one, and there are many applicants for it. I think you will like my friend, if he gets it."

"Like him!" I groaned.

The idea was horrible to me.

The ghost evidently perceived how deeply I was affected by what he had said, for there was a compassionate expression on his countenance. As I looked at him an idea struck me.   If I were to have any ghost at all about the house, I would prefer this one. Could there be such things as duplex ghost-ships?   Since it was day here when it was night in Russia, why could not this spectre serve in both places?   It was common enough for a person to fill two situations. The notion seemed feasible to me, and I broached it.

"Thank you," said the ghost.   "But the matter cannot be arranged in that way. Night and day are not suitably divided between here and Russia; and, besides, it is necessary for the incumbent of this place to be on duty at all hours.   You remember that I came to you by day as well as at night?"

Oh yes! I remembered that.   It was additionally unfortunate that the ghostship here should not be one of the limited kind.

"Why is it," I asked, "that a man's own spirit does not attend to these matters? I always thought that was the way the thing was managed."

The ghost shook his head.

"Consider for a moment," he replied, "what chance a man's own spirit, without experience and without influence, would have in a crowd of importunate applicants, versed in all the arts, and backed by the influence necessary in such a contest. Of course there are cases in which a person becomes his own ghost; but this is because the position is undesirable, and there is no competition."

"And this new-comer," I exclaimed, in much trouble, "will he take the form of Mr. Hinckman? If my wife should see such an apparition it would kill her."

"The ghost who will haunt this place," said my companion, "will not appear in the form of John Hinckman. I am glad that is so, if it will please you; for you are the only man with whom I have ever held such unrestrained and pleasant intercourse. Good-bye."

And with these words no figure of a Russian officer stood before me.

For some minutes I remained motionless, with downcast eyes, a very different man from the one who had just gazed out with such delight over the beautiful landscape. A shadow, not that of night, had fallen over everything. This fine estate was not to come to us clear and unencumbered, as we thought. It was to be saddled with a horrible lien, a spectral mortgage.

Madeline had gone upstairs with Pegram.

Pegram was our baby. I disliked his appellation with all my heart; but Pegram was a family name on Madeline's side of the house, and she insisted that our babe should bear it. Madeline was very much wrapped up in Pegram, often I thought too much so; for there were many times when I should have been very glad of my wife's society, but was obliged to do without it because she was entirely occupied with Pegram. To be sure, my wife's sister was with us, and there was a child's nurse; but, for all that, Madeline was so completely Pegramised, that a great many of the hours which I, in my anticipations of matrimonial felicity, had imagined would be passed in the company of my wife, were spent alone, or with the old gentleman, or Belle.

Belle was a fine girl; to me not so charming and attractive as her sister, but perhaps equally so to some other persons, certainly to one. This was Will Crenshaw, an old schoolfellow of mine, then a civil engineer, in South America. Will was the declared suitor of Belle, although she had never formally accepted him; but Madeline and myself both strongly favoured the match, and felt very anxious that she should do so, and indeed were quite certain that when

Will should return everything would be made all right. The young engineer was a capital fellow, had excellent prospects, and was my best friend. It was our plan that after their marriage the youthful couple should live with us. This, of course, would be delightful to both Belle and her sister, and I could desire no better companion than Will. He was not to go to distant countries any more, and who could imagine a pleasanter home than ours would be?

And now here was this dreadful prospect of a household ghost!

A week or so passed by, and John Hinckman was no more. Everything was done for him that respect and affection could dictate, and no one mourned his death more heartily than I. If I could have had my way he would have lived as long as I, myself, remained upon this earth.

When everything about the house had settled down into its accustomed quiet, I began to look out for the coming of the expected ghost. I felt sure that I would be the one to whom he would make his appearance, and with my regret and annoyance at his expected coming was mingled a feeling of curiosity to know in what form he would appear. He was not to come as John

Hinckman—that was the only bit of comfort in the whole affair.

But several weeks passed, and I saw no ghost; and I began to think that perhaps the aversion I had shown to having such an inmate of my household had had its effect, and I was to be spared the infliction. And now another subject occupied my thoughts. It was summer, the afternoons were pleasant, and on one of them I asked Belle to take a walk with me. I would have preferred Madeline, but she had excused herself, as she was very busy making what I presumed to be an altar-cloth for Pegram. It turned out to be an afghan for his baby carriage, but the effect was the same: she could not go. When I could not have Madeline I liked very well to walk with Belle. She was a pleasant girl, and in these walks I always talked to her of Crenshaw. My desire that she should marry my friend grew stronger daily. But this afternoon Belle hesitated, and looked a little confused.

"I am not sure that I shall walk to-day."

"But you have your hat on," I urged: "I supposed you had made ready for a walk."

"No," said she: "I thought I would go somewhere with my book."

"You haven't a book," I said, looking at her hands, one of which held a parasol.

"You are dreadfully exact," she replied, with a little laugh : "I am going into the library to get one." And away she ran.

There was something about this I did not like. I firmly believed she had come downstairs prepared to take a walk. But she did not want me ; that was evident enough. I went off for a long walk, and when I returned supper was ready, but Belle had not appeared.

"She has gone off somewhere with a book," I said. "I 'll go and look for her."

I walked down to the bosky grove at the foot of the lawn, and passed through it without seeing any signs of Belle. Soon, however, I caught sight of her light dress in an open space a little distance beyond me. Stepping forward a few paces I had a full view of her, and my astonishment can be imagined when I saw that she was standing in the shade of a tree talking to a young man. His back was turned toward me, but I could see from his figure and general air that he was young. His hat was a little on one side, in his hand he carried a short whip, and he wore a pair of riding-boots. He and Belle were engaged in very earnest conversation, and did not perceive me. I was not only surprised but shocked at the sight. I was quite certain Belle had come here to meet this young man, who, to me, was a total stranger. I did not wish Belle to know that I had seen her with him; and so I stepped back out of their sight, and began to call her. It was not long before I saw her coming toward me, and, as I expected, alone.

"Indeed," she cried, looking at her watch, "I did not know it was so late."

"Have you had a pleasant time with your book?" I asked, as we walked home-ward.

"I wasn't reading all the time," she answered.

I asked her no more questions. It was not for me to begin an inquisition into this matter. But that night I told Madeline all about it. The news troubled her much, and like myself she was greatly grieved at Belle's evident desire to deceive us. When there was a necessity for it, my wife could completely de-Pegramise herself, and enter with quick and judicious action into the affairs of others.

"I will go with her to-morrow," she said. "If this person comes, I do not intend that she shall meet him alone."

The next afternoon Belle started out again

with her book; but she had gone but a few
steps when she was joined by Madeline, with
hat and parasol, and together they walked
into the bosky grove. They returned in
very good time for supper; and as we went
in to that meal, Madeline whispered to me—

"There was nobody there."

"And did she say nothing to you of the
young man with whom she was talking yester-
day?" I asked, when we were alone some
hours later.

"Not a word," she said, "though I gave
her every opportunity. I wonder if you
could have been mistaken."

"I am sure I was not," I replied. "I saw
the man as plainly as I see you."

"Then Belle is treating us very badly,"
she said. "If she desires the company of
young men, let her say so, and we will invite
them to the house."

I did not altogether agree with this latter
remark. I did not care to have Belle know
young men. I wanted her to marry Will
Crenshaw, and be done with it. But we
both agreed not to speak to the young lady
on the subject. It was not for us to pry into
her secrets, and if anything was to be said
she should say it.

Every afternoon Belle went away, as before, with her book; but we did not accompany her, nor allude to her newly acquired love for solitary walks and studies. One afternoon we had callers, and she could not go. That night, after I had gone to sleep, Madeline awoke me with a little shake.

"Listen," she whispered. "Whom is Belle talking to?"

The night was warm, and all our doors and windows were open. Belle's chamber was not far from ours; and we could distinctly hear her speaking in a low tone. She was evidently holding a conversation with some one whose voice we could not hear.

"I'll go in," said Madeline, rising, "and see about this."

"No, no," I whispered. "She is talking to some one outside. Let me go down and speak to him."

I slipped on some clothes and stole quietly down the stairs. I unfastened the back door and went round to the side on which Belle's window opened. No sooner had I reached the corner than I saw, directly under the window, and looking upward, his hat cocked a good deal on one side, and his riding-whip in his hand, the jaunty young fellow with whom I had seen Belle talking.

"Hello!" I cried, and rushed toward him.

At the sound of my voice he turned to me, and I saw his face distinctly. He was young and handsome. There was a sort of half laugh on his countenance, as if he had just been saying something very witty. But he did not wait to finish his remark or to speak to me. There was a large evergreen near him ; and stepping quickly behind it, he was lost to my view. I ran around the bush, but could see nothing of him. There was a good deal of shrubbery hereabouts, and he was easily able to get away unobserved. I continued the search for about ten minutes, and then, quite sure that the fellow had got away, I returned to the house. Madeline had lighted a lamp, and was calling down-stairs to ask if I had found the man ; some of the servants were up, and anxious to know what had happened ; Pegram was crying ; but in Belle's room all was quiet. Madeline looked in at the open door, and saw her lying quietly in her bed. No word was spoken ; and my wife returned to our room, where we discussed the affair for a long time.

In the morning I determined to give Belle a chance to speak, and at the breakfast-table I said to her—

"I suppose you heard the disturbance last night?"

" Yes," she said quietly. " Did you catch the man ? "

" No," I answered, with considerable irritation, " but I wish I had."

" What would you have done if you had caught him ? " she asked, as with unusual slowness and deliberation she poured some cream upon her oat-meal.

" Done ! " I exclaimed, " I don't know what I would have done. But one thing is certain, I would have made him understand that I would have no strangers prowling around my house at night."

Belle coloured a little at the last part of this remark ; but she made no answer, and the subject was dropped.

This conversation greatly pained both Madeline and myself. It made it quite clear to us that Belle was aware that we knew of her acquaintance with this young man, and that she still determined to say nothing to us, either in the way of confidence or excuse. She had treated us badly, and we could not help showing it. On her side Belle was very quiet, and entirely different from the gay girl she had been some time before.

I urged Madeline to go to Belle, and speak to her as a sister, but she declined. " No," she said : " I know Belle's spirit, and there would be trouble. If there is to be a quarrel I shall not begin it."

I was determined to end this unpleasant feeling, which, to me, was almost as bad as a quarrel. If the thing were possible I would put an end to the young man's visits. I could never have the same opinion of Belle I had had before ; but if this impudent fellow could be kept away, and Will Crenshaw should come back and attend to his business as an earnest suitor ought, all might yet be well.

And now, strange to say, I began to long for the ghost, whose coming had been promised.   I had been considering what means I should take to keep Belle's clandestine visitor away, and had found the question rather a difficult one to settle. I could not shoot the man, and it would indeed be difficult to prevent the meeting of two young persons over whom I had no actual control. But I happened to think that if I could get the aid of the expected ghost the matter would be easy. If it should be as accommodating and obliging as the one who had haunted the house before, it would readily agree to forward the fortunes of the family by assisting in breaking up this unfortunate connection.   If it would consent to be present at their interviews the affair was settled. I knew from personal experience that love-making in the presence of a ghost was extremely unpleasant, and in this case I believed it would be impossible.

Every night, after the rest of the household had gone to bed, I wandered about the grounds, examining the porches and the balconies, looking up to the chimneys and the ornaments on the top of the house, hoping to see that phantom, whose coming I had, a short time before, anticipated with such dissatisfaction and repugnance. If I could even again meet the one who was now serving in Russia, I thought it would answer my purpose as well.

On the third or fourth night after I had begun my nocturnal rounds, I encountered, on a path not very far from the house, the young fellow who had given us so much trouble. My indignation at his impudent reappearance knew no bounds. The moon was somewhat obscured by fleecy clouds; but I could see that he wore the same jaunty air, his hat was cocked a little more on one side, he stood with his feet quite wide apart, and in his hands, clasped behind him, he held his riding-whip. I stepped quickly toward him.

"Well, sir!" I exclaimed.

He did not seem at all startled.

"How d' ye do?" he said, with a little nod.

"How dare you, sir," I cried, "intrude yourself on my premises? This is the second time I have found you here, and now I want you to understand that you are to get away from here just as fast as you can ; and if you are ever caught again anywhere on this estate, I 'll have you treated as a trespasser."

"Indeed," said he, "I would be sorry to put you to so much trouble. And now let me say that I have tried to keep out of your way, but since you have proved so determined to make my acquaintance I thought I might come forward and do the sociable."

"None of your impertinence," I cried. "What brings you here, anyway?"

"Well," said he, with a little laugh, "if you want to know, I don't mind telling you I came to see Miss Belle."

"You confounded rascal !" I cried, raising my heavy stick. "Get out of my sight, or I will break your head !"

"All right," said he, "break away !"

And drawing himself up, he gave his right boot a slap with his whip.

The whip went entirely through both legs! It was the ghost!

Utterly astounded, I started back, and sat down upon a raised flower-bed, against which I had stumbled. I had no strength, nor power to speak. I had seen a ghost before, but I was entirely overcome by this amazing development.

"And now I suppose you know who I am," said the spectre, approaching, and standing in front of me. "The one who was here before told me that your lady didn't fancy ghosts, and that I had better keep out of sight of both of you; but he didn't say anything about Miss Belle: and by George! sir, it wouldn't have mattered if he had; for if it hadn't been for that charming young lady I shouldn't have been here at all. I am the ghost of Buck Edwards, who was pretty well known in the lower part of this county about seventy years ago. I always had a great eye for the ladies, sir, and when I got a chance to court one I didn't miss it. I did too much courting, however; for I roused up a jealous fellow, named Ruggles, and he shot me in a duel early one September morning. Since then I have haunted, from time to time, more than a dozen houses where there were pretty girls."

"Do you mean to say," I asked, now finding strength, "that a spirit would care to come back to this earth to court a girl?"

"Why, what are you thinking of?" exclaimed the phantom of Buck Edwards. "Do you suppose that only old misers and lovelorn maidens want to come back and have a good time? No, sir! Every one of us, who is worth anything, comes if he can get a chance. By George, sir! do you know I courted Miss Belle's grandmother? And a couple of gay young ones we were, too! Nobody ever knew anything of it, and that made it all the livelier."

"Do you intend to stay here and pay attention to my sister-in-law?" I asked anxiously.

"Certainly I do," was the reply. "Didn't I say that is what I came for?"

"Don't you see the mischief you will do?" I asked. "You will probably break off a match between her and a most excellent gentleman whom we all desire "——

"Break off a match!" exclaimed the ghost of Buck Edwards, with a satisfied grin. "How many matches I have broken off! The last thing I ever did, before I went away, was of that sort. She wouldn't marry the gentleman who shot me." There was evidently no conscience to this spectre.

"And if you do not care for that," I said, in considerable anger, "I can tell you that you are causing ill-feeling between the young lady and the best friends she has in the world, which may end very disastrously."

"Now, look here, my man," said the ghost; "if you and your wife are really her friends, you won't act like fools and make trouble."

I made no answer to this remark, but asserted, with much warmth, that I intended to tell Miss Belle exactly what he was, and so break off the engagement at once.

"If you tell her that she's been walking and talking with the ghost of the fellow who courted her grandmother,—I reckon she could find some of my letters now among the old lady's papers if she looked for them, —you'd frighten the wits out of her. She'd go crazy. I know girls' natures, sir."

"So do I," I groaned.

"Don't get excited," he said. "Let the girl alone, and everything will be comfortable and pleasant. Good night."

I went to bed, but not to sleep. Here

was a terrible situation. A sister-in-law courted by a ghost! Was ever a man called upon to sustain such a trial! And I must sustain it alone. There was no one with whom I could share the secret.

Several times after this I saw this baleful spectre of a young buck of the olden time. He would nod to me with a jocular air, but I did not care to speak to him. One afternoon I went into the house to look for my wife; and, very naturally, I entered the room where Pegram lay in his little bed. The child was asleep, and no one was with him. I stood and gazed contemplatively upon my son. He was a handsome child, and apparently full of noble instincts; and yet I could not help wishing that he were older, or that in some way his conditions were such that it should not be necessary, figuratively speaking, that his mother should continually hover about him. If she could be content with a little less of Pegram and a little more of me, my anticipations of a matrimonial career would be more fully realised.

As these thoughts were passing through my mind I raised my eyes, and on the other side of the little bedstead I saw the wretched ghost of Buck Edwards.

"Fine boy," he said.

My indignation at seeing this impudent existence within the most sacred precincts of my house was boundless.

"You vile interloper!" I cried.

At this moment Madeline entered the room. Pale and stern, she walked directly to the crib and took up the child. Then she turned to me and said—

"I was standing in the doorway, and saw you looking at my babe. I heard what you said to him. I have suspected it before." And then, with Pegram in her arms, she strode out of the room.

The ghost had vanished as Madeline entered. Filled with rage and bitterness, for my wife had never spoken to me in these tones before, I ran downstairs and rushed out of the house. I walked long and far, my mind filled with doleful thoughts. When I returned to the house, I found a note from my wife. It ran thus—

"I have gone to Aunt Hannah's with Pegram, and have taken Belle. I cannot live with one who considers my child a vile interloper."

As I sat down in my misery, there was one little spark of comfort amid the gloom. She had taken Belle. My first impulse was to follow into the city and explain every-thing; but I quickly reflected that if I did this I must tell her of the ghost, and I felt certain that she would never return with Pegram to a haunted house. Must I, in order to regain my wife, give up this beautiful home? For two days I racked my brains and wandered gloomily about.

In one of my dreary rambles I encountered the ghost. "What are you doing here?" I cried. "Miss Belle has gone."

"I know that," the spectre answered, his air expressing all his usual impertinence and swagger, "but she'll come back. When your wife returns, she's bound to bring young Miss."

At this, a thought flashed through my mind. If any good would come of it, Belle should never return. Whatever else happened, this insolent ghost of a gay young buck should have no excuse for haunting my house.

"She will never come back while you are here," I cried.

"I don't believe it," it coolly answered.

I made no further assertions on the subject. I had determined what to do, and it was of no use to be angry with a vapouring creature like this. But I might as well get some information out of him.

"Tell me this," I asked; "if, for any

reason, you should leave this place and throw up your situation, so to speak, would you have a successor?"

"You needn't think I am going," it said contemptuously. "None of your little tricks on me. But I'll just tell you, for your satisfaction, that if I should take it into my head to cut the place, there would be another ghost here in no time."

"What is it," I cried, stamping my foot, "that causes this house to be so haunted by ghosts, when there are hundreds and thousands of places where such apparitions are never seen?"

"Old fellow," said the spectre, folding its arms, and looking at me with half-shut eyes, "it isn't the house that draws the ghosts, it is somebody in it; and as long as you are here the place will be haunted. But you needn't mind that. Some houses have rats, some have fever-and-ague, and some have ghosts. *Au revoir.*" And I was alone.

So then the spectral mortgage could never be lifted. With heavy heart and feet I passed through the bosky grove to my once happy home.

I had not been there half an hour when Belle arrived. She had come by the morning train, and had nothing with her but a little

hand-bag. I looked at her in astonishment.

"Infatuated girl," I cried, "could you not
stay away from here three days?"

"I am glad you said that," she answered,
taking a seat; "for now I think I am right
in suspecting what was on your mind. I ran
away from Madeline to see if I could find out
what was at the bottom of this dreadful
trouble between you. She told me what you
said, and I don't believe you ever used those
words to Pegram. And now I want to ask
you one question. Had I, in any way, anything to do with this?"

"No," said I, "not directly." And then,
emboldened by circumstances, I added:
"But that secret visitor or friend of yours
had much to do with it."

"I thought that might be so," she answered; "and now, George, I want to tell
you something, I am afraid it will shock you
very much."

"I have had so much to shock me lately
that I can stand almost anything now."

"Well then, it is this," she said. "That
person whom I saw sometimes, and whom
you once found under my window, is a
ghost."

"Did you know that?" I cried. "I

knew it was a ghost, but did not imagine
that you had any suspicion of it."

"Why, yes," she answered, "I saw
through him almost from the very first. I
was a good deal startled, and a little frightened when I found it out; but I soon felt
that this ghost couldn't do me any harm,
and you don't know how amusing it was.   I
always had a fancy for ghosts, but I never
expected to meet with one like this."

"And so you knew all the time it wasn't
a real man," I exclaimed, still filled with
astonishment at what I had heard.

"A real man!" cried Belle, with considerable contempt in her tones. "Do you
suppose I would become acquainted in that
way with a real man, and let him come
under my window and talk to me? I was
determined not to tell any of you about it;
for I knew you wouldn't approve of it, and
would break up the fun some way. Now I
wish most heartily that I had spoken of
it."

"Yes," I answered, "it might have
saved much trouble."

"But, O George!" she continued,
"you've no idea how funny it was! Such
a ridiculous, self-conceited, old-fashioned
ghost of a beau!"

"Yes," said I, "when it was alive it courted your grandmother."

"The impudence!" exclaimed Belle. "And to think that it supposed that I imagined it to be a real man! Why, one day, when it was talking to me, it stepped back into a rose-bush; and it stood there ever so long, all mixed up with the roses and leaves."

"And you knew it all the time?"

These words were spoken in a hollow voice by some one near us. Turning quickly, we saw the ghost of Buck Edwards, but no longer the jaunty spectre we had seen before. His hat was on the back of his head, his knees were turned inward, his shoulders drooped, his head hung, and his arms dangled limp at his sides.

"Yes," said Belle, "I knew it all the time."

The ghost looked at her with a faded, misty eye; and then, instead of vanishing briskly, as was his wont, he began slowly and irresolutely to disappear. First his body faded from view, then his head, leaving his hat and boots. These gradually vanished, and the last thing we saw of the once Buck Edwards was a dissolving view of the tip-end of a limp and drooping riding-whip.

"He is gone," said Belle.   "We 'll never see him again."

"Yes," said I, "he is gone. I think your discovery of his real nature has completely broken up that proud spirit. And now, what is to be done about Madeline?"

"Wasn't it the ghost you called an interloper?" asked Belle.

"Certainly it was," I replied.

"Well, then, go and tell her so," said Belle.

"About the ghost and all!" I exclaimed.

"Certainly," said she.

And together we went to Madeline, and I told her all. I found her with her anger gone, and steeped in misery. When I had finished, all Pegramed as she was, she plunged into my arms. I pressed my wife and child closely to my bosom, and we wept with joy.

When Will Crenshaw came home and was told this story, he said it didn't trouble him a bit.

"I 'm not afraid of a rival like that," he remarked. "Such a suitor wouldn't stand a ghost of a chance."

"But I can tell you," said Madeline, "that you had better be up and doing on your own account. A girl like Belle needn't be expected to depend on the chance of a ghost."

Crenshaw heeded her words, and the young couple were married in the fall. The wedding took place in the little church near our house. It was a quiet marriage, and was attended by a strictly family party. At the conclusion of the ceremonies I felt, or saw, for I am sure I did not hear—a little sigh quite near me.

I turned, and sitting on the chancel-steps I saw the spectre of Buck Edwards. His head was bowed, and his hands, holding his hat and riding-whip, rested carelessly on his knees.

"Bedad, sir!" he exclaimed, "to think of it! If I hadn't cut up as I did I might have married, and have been that girl's grandfather!"

The idea made me smile.

"It can't be remedied now," I answered.

"Such a remark to make at a wedding!" said Madeline, giving me a punch with her reproachful elbow.

THAT SAME OLD 'COON.

L or T.

WE were sitting on the store-porch of a small Virginia village. I was one of the party, and Martin Heiskill was the other one. Martin had been out fishing, which was an unusual thing for him.

"Yes, sir," said he, as he held up the small string of fish which he had laid carefully under his chair when he sat down to light his pipe; "that's all I've got to show for 'a day's work. But 'tain't often that I waste time that way. I don't b'lieve in huntin' fur a thing that ye can't see. If fishes sot on trees, now, and ye could shoot at 'em, I'd go out and hunt fishes with anybody. But it's mighty triflin' work to be goin' it blind in a mill-pond."

I ventured to state that there were fish that were occasionally found on trees. In India, for instance, a certain fish climbs trees.

"A which what's?" exclaimed Martin,

with an arrangement of pronouns peculiar
to himself.

"Oh yes !" he said, when I had told him
all I knew about this bit of natural history.
"That's very likely. I reckon they do that
up North, where you come from, in some of
them towns you was tellin' me about, where
there's so many houses that they tech each
other."

"That's all true about the fishes, Martin,"
said I, wisely making no reference to the
houses, for I did not want to push his belief
too hard ; "but we 'll drop them now."

"Yes," said he, "I think we 'd better."

Martin was a good fellow and no fool; but he
had not travelled much, and had no correct
ideas of cities, nor, indeed, of much of anything outside of his native backwoods. But
of those backwoods he knew more than any
other man I ever met. He liked to talk,
but he resented tall stories.

"Martin," said I, glad to change the
subject, "do you think there 'll be many
'coons about, this fall ?"

"About as many as common, I reckon,"
he answered. "What do you want to know
fur ?"

"I 'd like to go out 'coon-hunting," I
said ; "that's something I have never tried."

"Well," said he, "I don't s'pose your goin' will make much difference in the number of 'em, but, what's the good uv it? You'd better go 'possum-huntin'. You kin eat a 'possum."

"Don't you ever eat 'coons?" I asked.

"Eat 'coons!" he exclaimed, with contempt. "Why, there isn't a nigger in this county 'd eat a 'coon. They ain't fit to eat."

"I should think they'd be as good as 'possums," said I. "They feed on pretty much the same things, don't they?"

"Well, there ain't much difference, that way; but a 'possum's a mighty different thing from a 'coon, when ye come to eat him. A 'possum's more like a kind o' tree-pig. An' when he's cooked, he's sweeter than any Suckin'-pig you ever see. But a 'coon's more like a cat. Who'd eat cats?"

I was about to relate some city sausage stories, but I refrained.

"To be sure," continued Martin, "there's Col. Tibbs, who says he's eat 'coon-meat, and liked it fust-rate; but then ag'in, he says frogs is good to eat, so ye see there's no dependin' on what people say. Now, I know what I'm a-talkin' about; 'coons ain't fit fur human bein's to eat."

"What makes you hunt 'em, then?" I asked.

"Hunt 'em fur fun," said the old fellow, striking a lucifer match under his chair, to re-light his pipe. "Ef ye talk about vittles, that's one thing; an' ef ye talk about fun, that's another thing. An' I don't know now whether you'd think it was fun. I kinder think you wouldn't. I reckon it'd seem like pretty hard work to you."

"I suppose it would," I said; "there are many things that would be hard work to me that would be nothing but sport to an old hunter like you."

"You're right there, sir. You never spoke truer than that in your life. There's no man inside o' six counties that's hunted more 'n I have. I've been at it ever sence I was a youngster; an' I've got a lot o' fun out uv it,—more fun than anything else, fur that matter. You see, afore the war, people used to go huntin' more for real sport than they do now. An' 'twa'n't because there was more game in this country then than there is now, fur there wa'n't,—not half as much. There's more game in Virginny now than there's been any time this fifty years."

I expressed my surprise at this statement, and he continued—

"It all stands to reason, plain enough. Ef you don't kill them wild critters off, they 'll jist breed and breed, till the whole country gits full uv 'em. An' nobody had no time to hunt 'em durin' the war,—we was busy huntin' different game then, and sometimes we was hunted ourselves; an' sence then the most uv us has had to knuckle down to work,—no time fur huntin' when you 've got to do your own hoein' and ploughin',—or at least, a big part uv it. An' I tell ye that back there in the mountains there 's lots o' deer where nobody livin' about here ever saw 'em before, and as fur turkeys, and 'coons, and 'possums, there 's more an' more uv 'em ev'ry year, but as fur beavers,— them confounded chills-and-fever rep-tyles, —there 's jist millions uv 'em, more or less."

"Do beavers have chills and fever?" I asked wonderingly.

"No," said he, "I wish they did. But they give it to folks. There ain't nothin' on earth that 's raised the price o' quinine in this country like them beavers. Ye see they 've jist had the'r own way now, pretty much ever sence the war broke out, and they 've gone to work and built dams across pretty nigh all the cricks we got, and that floods the bottom-lands, uv course, and makes ma'shes and swamps, where they used to be fust-rate corn-land. Why, I tell ye, sir, down here on Colt's Creek there 's a beaver-dam a quarter uv a mile long, an' the water 's backed up all over everything. Ain't that enough to give a whole county the chills? An' it does it, too. Ef the people 'd all go and sit on that there dam, they 'd shake it down. I tell ye, sir, the war give us, in this country, a good many things we didn't want, and among 'em 's chills. Before the war, nobody never heard of sich things as chills round about hyar. 'Tain't on'y the beavers, nuther. When ye can't afford to hire more 'n three or four niggers to work a big farm, 'tain't likely ye kin do no ditchin', and all the branches and the ditches in the bottom-lands fills up, an' a feller's best corn-fields is pretty much all swamp, and his family has to live on quinine."

"I should think it would pay well to hunt and trap these beavers," I remarked.

"Well, so it does, sometimes," said Martin ; "but half the people ain't got no time. Now it 's different with me, because I 'm not a-farmin'. An' then it ain't every-body that kin git 'em. It takes a kind o' eddication to hunt beaver. But you was a-askin' about 'coons."

"Yes," I said. "I'd like to go 'coon-hunting."

"There's lots o' fun in it," said he, knocking the ashes out of his pipe, and putting up his cowhide boots on the top of the porch-railing in front of him.

"About two or three years afore the war, I went out on a 'coon-hunt, which was the liveliest hunt I ever see in all my life. I never had sich a good hunt afore nur never sence. I was a-livin' over in Powhattan, and the 'coon was Haskinses 'coon. They called him Haskinses 'coon, because he was 'most allus seen somewhere on ole Tom Haskinses farm. Tom's dead now, an' so is the 'coon; but the farm's thar, an' I'm here, so ye kin b'lieve this story, jist as ef it was printed on paper. It was the most confoundedest queer 'coon anybody ever see in all this whole world. An' the queerness was this: it hadn't no stripes to its tail. Now ye needn't say to me that no 'coon was ever that way, fur this 'coon was, an' that settles it. All 'coons has four or five brown stripes a-runnin' roun' their tails,— all 'cept this one 'coon uv Haskinses. An' what's more, this was the savagest 'coon anybody ever did see in this whole world. That's what sot everybody huntin' him; fur the savager a 'coon is, an' the more grit ther' is in him, the more 's the fun when he comes to fight the dogs—fur that 's whar the fun comes in.   An' ther' is 'coons as kin lick a whole pack o' dogs, an' git off; and this is jist what Haskinses 'coon did, lots o' times.   I b'lieve every nigger in the county, an' pretty much half the white men, had been out huntin' that 'coon, and they 'd never got him yit.   Ye see he was so derned cunnin' an' gritty, that when ye cut his tree down, he 'd jist go through the dogs like a wasp in a Sunday school, an' git away, as I tell ye.   He must a' had teeth more 'n an inch long, and he had a mighty tough bite to him.   Quick, too, as a black-snake.   Well, they never got him, no how; but he was often seed, fur he 'd even let a feller as hadn't a gun with him git a look at him in the day-time, which is contrary to the natur' of a 'coon, which keeps dark all day an on'y comes out arter dark.   But this here 'coon o' Haskinses was different from any 'coon anybody ever see in all this world.   Sometimes ye 'd see him a-settin' down by a branch, a-dippin' his food inter the water every time he took a bite, which is the natur' of a 'coon; but if ye put yer hand inter yer pocket fur so much as a pocket-pistol, he'd skoot afore ye could wink.

"Well, I made up my mind I'd go out after Haskinses 'coon, and I got up a huntin' party. 'Twa'n't no trouble to do that. In them days ye could git up a huntin' party easier than anything else in this whole world. All ye had to do was to let the people know, an' they'd be thar, black an' white. Why, I tell ye, sir, they used to go fox-huntin' a lot in them days, an' there wasn't half as many foxes as ther' is now, nuther. If a feller woke up bright an' early, an' felt like fox-huntin', all he had to do was to git on his horse, and take his dogs and his horn, and ride off to his nex' neighbour's, an' holler. An' up'd jump the nex' feller, and git on his horse, and take his dogs, and them two'd ride off to the nex' farm an' holler, an' keep that up till ther' was a lot uv 'em, with the'r hounds, and away they'd go, tip-it-ty-crack, after the fox an' the hounds—fur it didn't take long for them dogs to scar' up a fox. An' they'd keep it up, too, like good fellers. Ther' was a party uv 'em, once, started out of a Friday mornin', and the'r fox, which was a red fox (fur a grey fox ain't no good fur a long run) took 'em clean over into Albemarle, and none uv 'em didn't get back home till arter dark, Saturday. That was the way we used to hunt.

"Well, I got up my party, and we went out arter Haskinses 'coon. We started out pretty soon arter supper. Ole Tom Haskins himself was along, because, uv course, he wanted to see his 'coon killed; an' ther' was a lot of other fellers that you wouldn't know ef I was to tell ye the'r names. Ye see, it was 'way down at the lower end of the county that I was a-livin' then. An' ther' was about a dozen niggers with axes, an' five or six little black boys to carry light-wood. There was no less than thirteen dogs, all 'coon-hunters.

"Ye see, the 'coon-dog is sometimes a hound, an' sometimes he isn't. It takes a right smart dog to hunt a 'coon; and sometimes ye kin train a dog, thet ain't a reg'lar huntin'-dog, to be a fust-rate 'coon-dog, pertickerlerly when the fightin' comes in. To be sure, ye want a dog with a good nose to him to foller up a 'coon; but ye want fellers with good jaws and teeth, and plenty of grit, too. We had thirteen of the best 'coon-dogs in the whole world, an' that was enough fur any one 'coon, I say; though Haskinses 'coon was a pertickerler kind of a 'coon, as I tell ye.

"Pretty soon arter we got inter Haskinses oak woods, jist back o' the house, the dogs got on the track uv a 'coon, an' after 'em we all went, as hard as we could skoot. Uv course we didn't know that it was Haskinses 'coon we was arter; but we made up our minds, afore we started, thet when we killed a 'coon and found it wasn't Haskinses 'coon, we'd jist keep on till we did find him. We didn't 'spect to have much trouble a-findin' him, fur we know'd pretty much whar he lived, and we went right thar. 'Tain't often anybody hunts fur one pertickerler 'coon; but that was the matter this time, as I tell ye."

It 'was evident from the business-like way in which Martin Heiskill started into this story, that he wouldn't get home in time to have his fish cooked for supper, but that was not my affair. It was not every day that the old fellow chose to talk, and I was glad enough to have him go on as long as he would.

"As I tell ye," continued Martin, looking steadily over the toe of one of his boots, as if taking a long aim at some distant turkey, "we put off, hot and heavy, arter that ar 'coon, and hard work it was, too. The dogs took us down through the very stickeryest

part of the woods, and then down the holler
by the edge of Lumley's mill-pond,—whar
no human bein' in this world ever walked or
run afore, I truly b'lieve, fur it was the
meanest travellin' groun' I ever see,—and
then back inter the woods ag'in. But
'twa'n't long afore we came up to the dogs
a-barkin' and howlin' around a big chestnut-
oak about three foot through, an' we knew
we had him. That is, ef it wa'n't Haskinses
'coon. Ef it was his 'coon, may be we had
him, and may be we hadn't. The boys
lighted up their light-wood torches, and two
niggers with axes bent to work at the tree.
And them as wasn't choppin' had as much
as they could do to keep the dogs back out
o' the way o' the axes.

"The dogs they was jist goin' on as ef
they was mad, and ole Uncle Pete Williams
—he was the one thet was a-holdin' on to
Chink, the big dog—that dog's name was
Chinkerpin, an' he was the best 'coon dog in
the whole world, I reckon. He was a big
hound, brown an' black, an' he was the on'y
dog in thet pack thet had never had a fight
with Haskinses 'coon. They fetched him
over from Cumberland, a-purpose for this
hunt. Well, as I tell ye, ole Pete, says he,
'Thar ain't no mistook dis time, Mahsr

Tom, now I tell you. Dese yar dogs knows well 'nuf dat dat 'coon 's Mahsr Tom's 'coon, an' dey tell Chink too, fur he 's a-doin' de debbil's own pullin' dis time.' An' I reckon Uncle Pete was 'bout right, fur I thought the dog ud pull him off his legs afore he got through.

"Pretty soon the niggers hollered fur to stan' from under, an' down came the chestnut-oak with the big smash, an' then ev'ry dog an' man an' nigger made one skoot fur that tree. But they couldn't see no 'coon, fur he was in a hole 'bout half way up the trunk; an' then there was another high ole time keepin' back the dogs till the fellers with axes cut him out. It didn't take long to do that. The tree was a kind o' rotten up thar, and afore I know'd it, out hopped the 'coon; and then in less than half a shake, there was sich a fight as you never see in all this world.

"At first, it 'peared like it was a blamed mean thing to let thirteen dogs fight one 'coon; but pretty soon I thought it was a little too bad to have on'y thirteen dogs fur sich a fiery savage beast as that there 'coon was. He jist laid down on his back an' buzzed around like a coffee-mill, an' whenever a dog got a snap at him, he got the 'coon's teeth inter him quick as lightnin'. Ther' was too many dogs in that fight, an' 'twa'n't long before some uv 'em found that out, and got out o' the muss. An' it was some o' the dogs thet had the best chance at the 'coon thet left fust.

"Afore long, though, old Chink, who'd a been a-watchin' his chance, he got a good grip on that 'coon, an' that was the end of him. He jist throw'd up his hand.

"The minute I seed the fight was over, I rushed in an' grabbed that 'coon, an' like to got grabbed myself, too, in doin' it, 'specially by Chink, who didn't know me. One o' the boys brought a light-wood torch so's we could see the little beast.

"Well, 'twa'n't Haskinses 'coon. He had rings round his tail, jist as reg'lar as ef he was the feller that set the fashion. So ther' was more 'coon-huntin' to be done that night. But ther' wa'n't nobody that objected to that, fur we were jist gittin' inter the fun o' the thing. An' I made up my mind I wasn't a-goin' home without the tail off er Haskinses 'coon.

"I disremember now whether the nex' thing we killed was a 'coon or a 'possum. It's a long time ago, and I've been on lots o' hunts sence thet; but the main p'ints o' this hunt I ain't likely to furgit, fur, as I tell ye, this was the liveliest 'coon-hunt I ever went out on.

"Ef it was a 'possum we got next, ther' wasn't much fun about it, fur a 'possum's not a game beast. Ther's no fight in him, though his meat's better. When ye tree a 'possum an' cut down the tree, an' cut him out uv his hole, ef he's in one, he jist keels over an' makes b'lieve he's dead, though that's jinerally no use at all, fur he's real dead in a minute, and it's hardly wuth while fur him to take the trouble uv puttin' on the sham. Sometimes a 'possum 'll hang by his tail to the limb of a tree, an' ye kin knock him down without cuttin' the tree down., He's not a game beast, as I tell ye. But they ain't allus killed on the spot. I've seed niggers take a long saplin' an' make a little split in it about the middle of the pole, an' stick the end of a 'possum's long rat-tail through the split an' carry him home. I've seed two niggers carryin' a pole that a-way, one at each end, with two or three 'possums a-hanging frum it. They take 'em home and fatten 'em. I hate a 'possum, principally fur his tail. Ef it was curled up short, an' had a knot in it, it would be more like a pig's-tail, an' then it would seem as ef the

thing was meant to eat. But the way they
have it, it 's like nothing in the whole world
but a rat's tail.

"So, as I tell ye, ef thet was a 'possum
thet we treed nex', ther' wasn't no fight, an'
some of the niggers got some meat. But
after that—I remember it was about the
middle o' the night—we got off again,
this time really arter Haskinses 'coon. I
was dead sure of it. The dogs went
diff'rent, too. They was jist full o' fire
an' blood, an' run ahead like as ef they
was mad. They know'd they wasn't on the
track of no common 'coon, this time. As
fur all uv us men, black *an'* white, we jist
got up an' got arter them dogs, an some o'
the little fellers got stuck in a swamp, down
by a branch that runs out o' Haskinses
woods into Widder Thorp's corn-field; but
we didn't stop fur nuthin', an' they never
ketched up. We kep' on down that branch
an' through the whole corn-field, an' then the
dogs they took us crossways up a hill, whar
we had to cross two or three gullies, an' I
like to broke my neck down one uv 'em, fur
I was in sich a blamed hurry that I tried to
jump across, an' the bank giv' way on the
other side, as I might 'a' know'd it would,
an' down I come, backward. But I landed

on two niggers at the bottom of the gully,
an' that kinder broke my fall, an' I was up
an' a-goin' ag'in afore you 'd 'a' know'd it.

"Well, as I tell ye, we jist b'iled up that
hill, an' then we struck inter the widder's
woods, which is the wust woods in the whole
world, I reckon, fur runnin' through arter a
pack o' dogs. The whole place was so
growed up with chinkerpin-bushes and dog-
wood, an' every other kind o' underbrush
that a hog would 'a' sp'iled his temper goin'
through thar in the day-time; but we jist
r'ared an' plunged through them bushes right
on to the tails o' the dogs; an' ef any uv us
had had good clothes on, they 'd 'a' been
tore off our backs. But ole clothes won't
tear, an' we didn't care ef they did. The
dogs had a hot scent, an' I tell ye, we was
close on to 'em when they got to the critter.
An' what d 'ye s'pose the critter was? It was
a dog-arned 'possum in a trap!

"It was a trap sot by ole Uncle Enoch
Peters, that lived on Widder Thorp's farm.
He 's dead now, but I remember him fust-
rate. He had an' ole mother over in Cumberland, an' he was the very oldest man in
this country, an' I reckon in the whole
world, that had a livin' mother. Well, that
there sneakin' 'possum had gone snifflin'

along through the corn-field, an' up that hill, an' along the gullies, and through that onearthly woods to Uncle Enoch's trap, an' we'd follered him as ef he'd had a store order fur a bar'l o' flour tied to his tail.

"Well, he didn't last long, for the dogs and the niggers, between 'em, tore that trap all to bits; and what become o' the 'possum I don't b'lieve anybody knowed, 'cept it was ole Chink and two or three uv the biggest dogs."

I here asked if 'coons were ever caught in traps.

"Certainly they is," said Martin. "I remember the time that ther' was a good many 'coons caught in traps. That was in the ole Henry Clay 'lection times. The 'coon, he was the Whig beast. He stood for Harry Clay and the hull Whig party. Ther' never was a pole-raisin', or a barbecue, or a speech meetin', or a torchlight percession, in the whole country, that they didn't want a live 'coon to be sot on a pole or somewhar whar the people could look at him an' be encouraged. But it didn't do 'em no good. Ole Harry Clay he went under, an' ye couldn't sell a 'coon for a dime.

"Well, as I tell ye, this was a 'possum in a trap, and we was all pretty mad and pretty tired.   We got out on the edge o' the woods as soon as we could, an' thar was a field o' corn.   The corn had been planted late, and the boys found a lot o' roastin' ears, though they was purty old, but we didn't care for that.   We made a fire, an' roasted the corn, an' some o' the men had their 'ticklers' along,—enough to give us each a taste,—an' we lighted our pipes and sat down to take a rest afore startin' off ag'in arter Haskinses 'coon."

"But I thought you said," I remarked, "that you knew you were after Haskins' 'coon the last time."

"Well, so we did know we was.   But sometimes you know things as isn't so. Didn't'ye ever find that out? It's so, anyway, jist as I tell ye," and then he continued his story—   .

"As we was a-settin' aroun' the fire a-smokin' away, Uncle Pete Williams—he was the feller that had to hang on to the big dog Chink, as I tell ye—he come an' he says, 'Now, look-a-here, Mahsr Tom, an' de rest ob you all, don't ye bleab we'd better gib up dis yere thing an' go home?' Well, none uv us thought that, an' we told him so ; but he kep' on, an' begun to tell us we'd find ourselves in a heap o' misery, ef we didn't

look out, pretty soon. Says he : 'Now,
look-a-here, Mahsr Tom, and you all, you
all wouldn't a-ketched me out on this yere
hunt ef I'd 'a' knowed ye was a-gwine to hunt
'possums.   'Tain't no luck to hunt 'possums :
everybody knows dat. De debbil gits after
a man as will go a-chasin' 'possums wid dogs
when he kin cotch 'em a heap mau comfort-
abler in a trap.   'Tain't so much diff'rence
'bout 'coons, but the debbil he takes care o'
'possums. An' I 'spect de debbil know'd
'bout dis yere hunt, fur de oder ebenin' I was
a-goin' down to de rock-spring, wid a gourd
to git a drink, and dar on de rock, wid his
legs a-danglin' down to de water, sat de
debbil hisself a-chawin' green terbacker !'—
'Green terbacker?' says I. 'Why, Uncle
Pete, ain't the debbil got no better sense than
that?'—'Now, look-a-here, Mahsr Martin,'
says he, 'de debbil knows what he 's about,
an' ef green terbacker was good fur anybody
to chaw he wouldn't chaw it, an' he says to
me, "Uncle Pete, been a-huntin' any
'possums?" An' says I, "No, Mahsr, I
nebber do dat." An' den he look at me
awful, fur I seed he didn't furgit nothin', an'
he was a-sottin' dar, a-shinen as ef he was
polished all over wid shoe-blackin', an' he
says, "Now, look-a-here Uncle Pete, don't

you eber do it ; an' w'at's dat about dis yere Baptis' church at de Cross-roads, dat was sot afire ?" An' I tole him dat I didn't know nuffin' 'bout dat—not one single word in dis whole world. Den he wink, an' he says, "Dem bruders in dat church hunt too many 'possums. Dey is allus a-huntin' 'possums, an' dat's de way dey lose der church. I sot dat church afire mesef. D'y' hear dat, Uncle Pete?" An' I was glad enough to hear it, too ; for der was bruders in dat church dat said Yeller Joe an' me sot it afire, cos we wasn't 'lected trustees, but dey can't say dat now, fur it's all plain as day-light, an' ef dey don't bleab it, I kin show 'em de berry gourd I tuk down to de rock-spring when I seed de debbil. An' it don't do to hunt no more 'possums, fur de debbil 'd jist as leab scratch de end ob his tail ag'in a white man's church as ag'in a black man's church.'

"By this time we was all ready to start ag'in ; an' we know'd that all Uncle Pete wanted was to git home ag'in, fur he was lazy, and was sich an ole rascal that he was afraid to go back by himself in the dark fur fear the real debbil 'd gobble him up, an' so we didn't pay no 'tention to him, but jist started off ag'in. Ther' is niggers as b'lieve

the debbil gits after people that hunt
'possums, but Uncle Pete never b'lieved that
when he was a-goin' to git the 'possum.
Ther' wasn't no chance fur him this night,
but he had to come along all the same, as I
tell ye.

"'Twa'n't half an hour arter we started
ag'in afore we found a 'coon, but 'twa'n't
Haskinses 'coon. We was near the crick,
when the dogs got arter him, an' inste'd o'
gittin' up a tree, he run up inter the roots
uv a big pine thet had been blown down,
and was a-layin' half in the water. The
brush was mighty thick jist here ; an' some
uv us thought it was another 'possum, an'
we kep' back most uv the dogs, fur we didn't
want 'em to carry us along that creek-bank
arter no 'possum. But some o' the niggers,
with two or three dogs, pushed through the
bushes, and one feller clum up inter the roots
uv the tree, an' out jumped Mr. 'Coon. He
hadn't no chance to git off any other way ·
than to clim' down some grape-vines that
was a-hangin' from the tree inter the water.
So he slips down one o' them, an' as he was
a-hangin' on like a sailor a-goin' down a
rope, I got a look at him through the bushes,
an' I see plain enough by the light-wood
torch thet he wa'n't Haskinses 'coon. He

had the commonest kinds o' bands on his tail.

"Well, that thar 'coon he looked like he was about the biggest fool uv a 'coon in this whole world. He come down to the water, as ef he thought a dog couldn't swim, an' ef that 's what he did think he foun' out his mistake as soon as he teched the water, fur thar was a dog ready fur him. An' then they had it lively, an' the other dogs they jumped in, an' thar was a purty big splashin' an' plungin' an' bitin' in that thar creek ; an' I was jist a-goin' to push through an' holler fur the other fellers to come an' see the fun, when that thar 'coon he got off ! He jist licked them dogs—the meanest dogs we had along—an' put fur the other bank, an' that was the end o' him. 'Coons is a good deal like folks—it don't pay to call none uv 'em fools till ye 're done seein' what they 're up to.

"Well, as I tell ye, we was then nigh the crick ; but soon as we lef' the widder's woods we struck off from it, fur none uv us, 'specially the niggers, wanted to go nigh 'Lijah Parker's. Reckon ye don't know 'Lijah Parker. Well, he lives 'bout three mile from here on the crick ; an' he was then, an' is now, jist the laziest man in the whole world. He had two or three big red

oaks on his place thet he wanted cut down,
but was too durned lazy to do it; an' he
hadn't no money to hire anybody to do it,
nuther, an' he was too stingy to spend it ef
he 'd had it. So he know'd ther' was a-goin'
to be a 'coon-hunt one night; an' the evenin'
before he tuk a 'coon his boy 'd caught in a
'possum-trap, an' he put a chain aroun' its
body, and pulled it through his woods to
one of his red oak trees. Then he let the
'coon climb up a little ways, an' then he
jerked him down ag'in, and pulled him over
to another tree, and so on, till he 'd let him
run up three big trees. Then his boy got a
box, an' they put the 'coon in an' carried
him home. Uv course, when the dogs come
inter his woods—an' he know'd they was a-
goin' to do that—they got on the scent o'
this 'coon; an' when they got to the fust
tree, they thought they 'd treed him, an'
the niggers cut down that red oak in no
time. An' then, when ther' wa'n't no 'coon
thar, they tracked him to the nex' tree, an'
so on till the whole three trees was cut down.
We wouldn't 'a' found out nuthin' about this
ef 'Lijah's boy hadn't told on the ole man,
an' ye kin jist bet all ye 're wuth that ther'
ain't a man in this county that 'u'd cut one
o' his trees down ag'in.

" Well, as I tell ye, we kep' clear o' Parker's place, an' we walked about two mile, an' then we found we'd gone clean around till we'd got inter Haskinses woods ag'in. We hadn't gone further inter the woods than ye could pitch a rock afore the dogs got on the track uv a 'coon, an' away we all went arter 'em. Even the little fellers that was stuck in the swamp away back was with us now, fur they got out an' was a-pokin' home through the woods. 'Twa'n't long afore that 'coon was treed; an' when we got up an' looked at the tree, we all felt dead sure it was Haskinses 'coon this time, an' no mistake. Fur it was jist the kind o' tree that no 'coon but that 'coon would éver 'a' thought o' climbin'. Mos' 'coons and 'possums shin it up a pretty tall tree, to get as fur away frum the dogs as they kin, an' the tall trees is often purty slim trees, an' easy cut down. But this here 'coon o' Haskinses he had more sense than that. He jist skooted up the thickest tree he could find. He didn't care about gittin' up high. He know'd the dogs couldn't climb no tree at all, an' that no man or boy was a-comin' up after him. So he wanted to give 'em the best job o' choppin' he know'd how. Ther' ain't no smarter

critter than 'coons in this whole world.
Dogs ain't no circumstance to 'em. About
four or five year ago, I was a-livin' with
Riley Marsh, over by the Court-house; an'
his wife she had a tame 'coon, an' this little
beast was a mighty lot smarter than any
human bein' in the house. Sometimes, when
he'd come it a little too heavy with his
tricks, they used to chain him up, but he
always got loose and come a humpin' inter
the house with a bit o' the chain to his
collar. D'ye know how a 'coon walks? He
never comes straight ahead like a Christian,
but he humps up his back, an' he twists
roun' his tail, an' he sticks out his head,
crooked like, frum under his ha'r, an' he
comes inter a room sideways an' a kind o'
cross, as ef he'd a-wanted ter stay out an'
play, an' ye'd made him come in the house
ter learn his lessons.

"Well, as I tell ye, this 'coon broke his
chain ev'ry time, an' it was a good thick
dog-chain, an' that puzzled Riley; but one
day he saw the little runt goin' aroun' an'
aroun' hoppin' over his chain ev'ry time, till
he got an awful big twist on his chain, an'
then it was easy enough to strain on it till a
link opened. But Riley put a swivel on his
chain, an' stopped that fun. But they'd let

him out purty often; an' one day he squirmed himself inter the kitchen, an' thar he see the tea-kittle a-settin' by the fire-place. The lid was off, an' ole 'cooney thought that was jist the kind uv a black hole he 'd been used to crawlin' inter afore he got tame. So he crawled in an' curled himself up an' went to sleep. Arter a while, in comes Aunt Hannah to git supper; an' she picks up the kittle, an' findin' it heavy, thinks it was full o' water, an' puts on the lid an' hung it over the fire. Then she clapped on some light-wood to hurry up things. Purty soon that kittle began to warm; an' then, all uv a sudden, off pops the lid, an' out shoots Mister 'Coon like a rocket. An' ther' never was, in all this whole world, sich a frightened ole nigger as Aunt Hannah. She thought it was the debbil, sure, an' she giv' a yell that fetched ev'ry man on the place. That ere 'coon had more mischief in him than any live thing ye ever see. He 'd pick pockets, hide ev'ry thing he could find, an' steal eggs. He 'd find an egg ef the hen 'u'd sneak off an' lay it at the bottom uv the crick. One Sunday, Riley's wife went to all-day preachin' at Hornorsville, an' she put six mockin'-birds she was a-raisin' in one cage; an', fur fear

the 'coon 'u'd get 'em, she hung the cage
frum a hook in the middle uv the ceilin' in
the chamber. She had to 'git upon a chair to
do it. Well, she went to preachin', an' that
'coon he got inter the house an' eat up ev'ry
one o' them mockin'-birds. Ther' wasn't no
tellin' 'xactly how he done it ; but we
reckoned he got up on the high mantel-piece
an' made one big jump from thar to the cage,
an' hung on till he put his paw through an'
hauled out one bird. Then he dropped an'
eat that, an' made anuther jump, till they
was all gone. Anyway, he got all the birds,
an' that was the last meal he ever eat.

"Well, as I tell ye, that 'coon he got inter
the thickest tree in the whole woods ; an'
thar he sat a-peepin' at us from a crotch
that wasn't twenty feet frum the ground.
Young Charley Ferris he took a burnin'
chunk that one o' the boys had fetched along
frum the fire, an' throw'd it up at him, 'at
we could all see him plain. He was Haskinses 'coon, sure. There wasn't a stripe on
his tail. Arter that, the niggers jist made
them axes swing, I tell ye. They had a big
job afore 'em ; but they took turns at it, an'
didn't waste no time. An' the rest uv us, we
got the dogs ready. We wasn't a-goin' to
let this 'coon off this here time. No, sir ?

Ther' was too many dogs, as I tell ye, an' we had four or five uv the clumsiest uv 'em tuk a little way off, with boys to hole 'em; an' the other dogs an' the hounds, 'specially old Chink, was held ready to tackle the 'coon when the time come. An' we had to be mighty sharp about this, too, fur we all saw that that thar 'coon was a-goin' to put the minute the tree come down. He wasn't goin' to git in a hole an' be cut out. Ther' didn't 'pear to be any hole, an' he didn't want none. All he wanted was a good thick tree an' a crotch to set in an' think. That was what he was a-doin'. He was cunjerin' up some trick or other. We all know'd that, but we jist made up our minds to be ready fur him; an' though, as he was Haskinses 'coon, the odds was ag'in us, we was dead sure we 'd git him this time.

"I thought that thar tree never *was* a-comin' down; but purty soon it began to crack and lean, and then down she come. Ev'ry dog, man, and boy, made a rush fur that crotch, but ther' was no coon thar. As the tree come down he seed how the land lay; and quicker 'n any light'in' in this whole world he jist streaked the other way to the root o' the tree, giv' one hop over the stump, an' was off. I seed him do it, an' the dogs see him, but they wasn't quick enough, and couldn't stop 'emselves—they was goin' so hard fur the crotch.

"'Ye never did see in all yer days sech a mad crowd as that thar crowd around that tree, but they didn't stop none to sw'ar. The dogs was arter the 'coon, an' arter him we went too. He put fur the edge of the woods, which looked queer, fur a 'coon never will go out into the open if he kin help it; but the dogs was so hot arter him that he couldn't run fur, and he was treed ag'in in less than five minutes. This time he was in a tall hick'ry-tree, right on the edge o' the woods; and it wa'n't a very thick tree, nuther; so the niggers they jist tuk ther' axes, but afore they could make a single crack, ole Haskins he runs at 'em an' pushes 'em away.

"''Don't ye touch that thar tree!' he hollers. 'That hick'ry marks my line!' An' sure enough, that was the tree with the surveyors' cuts on it, that marked the place where the line took a corner that run atween Haskinses farm and Widder Thorp's. He know'd the tree the minute he seed it, an' so did I, fur I carried the chain for the surveyors when they laid off the line; an' we could all see the cut they'd blazed on it, fur it was fresh yit, an' it was gittin' to be daylight now, an' we could see things plain.

"Well, as I tell ye, ev'ry man uv us jist r'ared and snorted, an' the dogs an' boys was madder'n the rest uv us, but ole Haskins he didn't give in. He jist walked aroun' that tree an' wouldn't let a nigger touch it. He said he wanted to kill the 'coon jist as much as anybody, but he wasn't a-goin to have his line sp'iled, arter the money he'd spent, fur all the 'coons in this whole world.

"Now did ye ever hear of sich a 'cute trick as that? That thar 'coon he must 'a' knowed that was Haskinses line-tree, an' I 'spect he'd 'a' made fur it fust, ef he'd a-knowed ole Haskins was along. But he didn't know it, till he was a-settin' in the crotch uv the big tree and could look aroun' an' see who was thar. It wouldn't 'a' been no use fur him to go for that hick'ry if Haskins hadn't 'a' bin thar, for he know'd well enough it 'u'd 'a' come down sure."

I smiled at this statement, but Martin shook his head.

"'Twon't do," he said, "to undervally the sense of no' coon. How're ye goin' to tell what he knows? Well, as I tell ye, we was jist gittin' madder an' madder when a nigger named Wash Webster, he run out in the field,—it was purty light now, as I tell ye—an' he hollers, ' O Mahsr Tom ! Mahsr Tom ! Dat ar 'coon he ain't you 'coon ! He got stripes to he tail !'

"We all made a rush out inter the field, to try to git a look ; an' sure enough we could see the little beast a-settin' up in a crotch over on that side, an' I do b'lieve he knowed what we was all a-lookin' up fur, fur he jist kind a lowered his tail out o' the crotch so 's we could see it, an' thar it was, striped, jist like any other 'coon's tail."

" And you were so positively sure this time, that it was Haskins' 'coon," I said. "Why, you saw, when the man threw the blazing chunk into the big tree, that it had no bands on its tail."

" That 's so," said Martin ; " but ther' ain't no man that kin see 'xactly straight uv a dark mornin', with no light but a flyin' chunk, an' 'specially when he wants to see somethin' that isn't thar. An' as to bein' certain about that 'coon, I jist tell ye that ther 's nuthin' a man 's more like to be mistook about, than a thing he knows fur dead sure.

" Well, as I tell ye, when we seed that that thar 'coon wa'n't Haskinses 'coon arter all, an' that we couldn't git him out er that tree as long as the ole man was thar, we jist give up and put across the field for Haskinses house, whar we was a-goin' to git breakfus'. Some of the boys and the dogs staid aroun' the tree, but ole Haskins he ordered 'em off an' wouldn't let nobody stay thar, though they had a mighty stretchin'-time gittin' the dogs away."

"It seems to me," said I, "that there wasn't much profit in that hunt."

"Well," said Martin, putting his pipe in his pocket, and feeling under his chair for his string of fish, which must have been pretty dry and stiff by this time, "the fun in a 'coon hunt ain't so much in gittin' the 'coon, as goin' arter him—which is purty much the same in a good many other things, as I tell ye."

And he took up his fish and departed.

HIS WIFE'S DECEASED SISTER.

HIS WIFE'S DECEASED SISTER.

IT is now five years since an event occurred
which so coloured my life, or rather so
changed some of its original colours, that
I have thought it well to write an account
of it, deeming that its lessons may be of
advantage to persons whose situations in life
are similar to my own.

When I was quite a young man I adopted
literature as a profession ; and having passed
through the necessary preparatory grades, I
found myself, after a good many years of
hard, and often unremunerative work, in
possession of what might be called a fair
literary practice. My articles, grave, gay,
practical, or fanciful, had come to be considered with a favour by the editors of the
various periodicals for which I wrote, on
which I found in time I could rely with a
very comfortable certainty. My productions
created no enthusiasm in the reading public ;
they gave me no great reputation or very
valuable pecuniary return ; but they were

always accepted, and my receipts from them, at the time to which I have referred, were as regular and reliable as a salary, and quite sufficient to give me more than a comfortable support.

It was at this time I married. I had been engaged for more than a year, but had not been willing to assume the support of a wife until I felt that my pecuniary position was so assured that I could do so with full satisfaction to my own conscience. There was now no doubt in regard to this position, either in my mind or in that of my wife. I worked with great steadiness and regularity; I knew exactly where to place the productions of my pen, and could calculate, with a fair degree of accuracy, the sums I should receive for them. We were by no means rich; but we had enough, and were thoroughly satisfied and content.

Those of my readers who are married will have no difficulty in remembering the peculiar ecstasy of the first weeks of their wedded life. It is then that the flowers of this world bloom brightest; that its sun is the most genial; that its clouds are the scarcest; that its fruit is the most delicious; that the air is the most balmy; that its cigars are of the highest flavour; that the warmth and radiance of early matrimonial felicity so rarefies the intellectual atmosphere, that the soul mounts higher, and enjoys a wider prospect, than ever before.

These experiences were mine. The plain claret of my mind was changed to sparkling champagne, and at the very height of its effervescence I wrote a story. The happy thought that then struck me for a tale was of a very peculiar character; and it interested me so much that I went to work at it with great delight and enthusiasm, and finished it in a comparatively short time. The title of the story was "His Wife's Deceased Sister;" and when I read it to Hypatia she was delighted with it, and at times was so affected by its pathos that her uncontrollable emotion caused a sympathetic dimness in my eyes, which prevented my seeing the words I had written. When the reading was ended, and my wife had dried her eyes, she turned to me and said, "This story will make your fortune. There has been nothing so pathetic since Lamartine's 'History of a Servant-Girl.'"

As soon as possible the next day I sent my story to the editor of the periodical for which I wrote most frequently, and in which my best productions generally appeared.

In a few days I had a letter from the editor, in which he praised my story as he had never before praised anything from my pen. It had interested and charmed, he said, not only himself, but all his associates in the office. Even old Gibson, who never cared to read anything until it was in proof, and who never praised anything which had not a joke in it, was induced by the example of the others to read this manuscript, and shed, as he asserted, the first tears that had come from his eyes since his final paternal castigation some forty years before. The story would appear, the editor assured me, as soon as he could possibly find room for it.

If anything could make our skies more genial, our flowers brighter, and the flavour of our fruit and cigars more delicious, it was a letter like this. And when, in a very short time, the story was published, we found that the reading public was inclined to receive it with as much sympathetic interest and favour as had been shown to it by the editors. My personal friends soon began to express enthusiastic opinions upon it. It was highly praised in many of the leading newspapers; and, altogether, it was a great literary success. I am not inclined to be vain of my writings, and, in general, my wife tells me, think too little of them ; but I did feel a good deal of pride and satisfaction in the success of "His Wife's Deceased Sister." If it did not make my fortune, as my wife asserted that it would, it certainly would help me very much in my literary career.

In less than a month from the writing of this story, something very unusual and un-expected happened to me. A manuscript was returned by the editor of the periodical in which "His Wife's Deceased Sister" had appeared. "It is a good story," he wrote, "but not equal to what you have just done. You have made a great hit; and it would not do to interfere with the reputation you have gained by publishing anything inferior to 'His Wife's Deceased Sister,' which has had such a deserved success."

I was so unaccustomed to having my work thrown back on my hands, that I think I must have turned a little pale when I read the letter. I said nothing of the matter to my wife, for it would be foolish to drop such grains of sand as this into the smoothly oiled machinery of our domestic felicity ; but I immediately sent the story to another editor. I am not able to express the astonishment I felt, when, in the course of a week, it was sent back to me. The tone of the note accompanying ⎜it indicated a somewhat injured feeling on the part of the editor. "I am reluctant," he said, "to decline a manuscript from you; but you know very well that if you sent me anything like 'His Wife's Deceased Sister' it would be most promptly accepted."

I now felt obliged to speak of the affair to my wife, who was quite as much surprised, though, perhaps, not quite as much shocked, as I had been.

"Let us read the story again," she said, "and see what is the matter with it." When we had finished its perusal, Hypatia remarked: "It is quite as good as many of the stories you have had printed, and I think it very interesting; although, of course, it is not equal to 'His Wife's Deceased Sister.'"

"Of course not," said I, "that was an inspiration that I cannot expect every day. But there must be something wrong about this last story which we do not perceive. Perhaps my recent success may have made me a little careless in writing it."

"I don't believe that," said Hypatia.

"At any rate," I continued, "I will lay it aside, and will go to work on a new one."

In due course of time I had another manuscript finished, and I sent it to my favourite periodical. It was retained some weeks, and then came back to me. "It will never do," the editor wrote, quite warmly, "for you to go backward. The demand for the number containing 'His Wife's Deceased Sister' still continues, and we do not intend to let you disappoint that great body of readers who would be so eager to see another number containing one of your stories."

I sent this manuscript to four other periodicals, and from each of them was it returned with remarks to the effect that, although it was not a bad story in itself, it was not what they would expect from the author of "His Wife's Deceased Sister."

The editor of a Western magazine wrote to me for a story to be published in a special number which he would issue for the holidays. I wrote him one of the character and length he asked for, and sent it to him. By return mail it came back to me. "I had hoped," the editor wrote, "when I asked for a story from your pen, to receive something like 'His Wife's Deceased Sister,' and I must own that I am very much disappointed."

I was so filled with anger when I read this

uote, that I openly objurgated "His Wife's Deceased Sister." "You must excuse me," I said to my astonished wife, "for expressing myself thus in your presence; but that confounded story will be the ruin of me yet. Until it is forgotten nobody will ever take anything I write."

"And you cannot expect it ever to be forgotten," said Hypatia, with tears in her eyes.

It is needless for me to detail my literary efforts in the course of the next few months. The ideas of the editors with whom my principal business had been done, in regard to my literary ability, had been so raised by my unfortunate story of "His Wife's Deceased Sister," that I found it was of no use to send them anything of lesser merit. And as to the other journals which I tried, they evidently considered it an insult for me to send them matter inferior to that by which my reputation had lately risen. The fact was that my successful story had ruined me. My income was at an end, and want actually stared me in the face; and I must admit that I did not like the expression of its countenance. It was of no use for me to try to write another story like "His Wife's Deceased Sister." I could not get married every time I began a new manuscript, and it was the exaltation of mind caused by my wedded felicity which produced that story.

"It's perfectly dreadful!" said my wife. "If I had had a sister, and she had died, I would have thought it was my fault."

"It could not be your fault," I answered, "and I do not think it was mine. I had no intention of deceiving anybody into the belief that I could do that sort of thing every time, and it ought not to be expected of me. Suppose Raphael's patrons had tried to keep him screwed up to the pitch of the Sistine Madonna, and had refused to buy anything which was not as good as that. In that case I think he would have occupied a much earlier and narrower grave than that on which Mr. Morris Moore hangs his funeral decorations."

"But my dear," said Hypatia, who was posted on such subjects, "the Sistine Madonna was one of his latest paintings."

"Very true," said I; "but if he had married, as I did, he would have painted it earlier."

I was walking homeward one afternoon about this time, when I met Barbel,—a man I had known well in my early literary career.   He was now about fifty years of age, but looked older.   His hair and beard were quite grey ; and his clothes, which were of the same general hue, gave me the idea that they, like his hair, had originally been black.   Age is very hard on a man's external appointments.   Barbel had an air of having been to let for a long time, and quite out of repair.   But there was a kindly gleam in his eye, and he welcomed me cordially.

"Why, what is the matter, old fellow?" said he.   "I never saw you look so wo-begone."

I had no reason to conceal anything from Barbel.   In my younger days he had been of great use to me, and he had a right to know the state of my affairs.   I laid the whole case plainly before him.

"Look here," he said, when I had fin-ished, "come with me to my room : I have something I would like to say to you there."

I followed Barbel to his room.   It was at the top of a very dirty and well-worn house, which stood in a narrow and lumpy street, into which few vehicles ever penetrated, ex-cept the ash and garbage carts, and the rickety wagons of the venders of stale vegetables.

"This is not exactly a fashionable promenade," said Barbel, as we approached the house; "but in some respects it reminds me of the streets in Italian towns, where the palaces lean over towards each other in such a friendly way."

Barbel's room was, to my mind, rather more doleful than the street. It was dark, it was dusty, and cobwebs hung from every corner. The few chairs upon the floor, and the books upon a greasy table, seemed to be afflicted with some dorsal epidemic, for their backs were either gone or broken. A little bedstead in the corner was covered with a spread made of *New York Heralds* with their edges pasted together.

"There is nothing better," said Barbel, noticing my glance towards this novel counterpane, "for a bedcovering than newspapers: they keep you as warm as a blanket, and are much lighter. I used to use *Tribunes*, but they rattled too much."

The only part of the room which was well lighted was at one end near the solitary window. Here, upon a table with a spliced leg, stood a little grindstone.

"At the other end of the room," said Barbel, "is my cook-stove, which you can't see unless I light the candle in the bottle which stands by it; but if you don't care particularly to examine it, I won't go to the expense of lighting up. You might pick up a good many odd pieces of bric-a-brac around here, if you chose to strike a match and investigate ; but I would not advise you to do so. It would pay better to throw the things out of the window than to carry them downstairs. The particular piece of indoor decoration to which I wish to call your attention is this." And he led me to a little wooden frame which hung against the wall near the window. Behind a dusty piece of glass it held what appeared to be a leaf from a small magazine or journal. "There," said he, "you see a page from *The Grasshopper*, a humorous paper which flourished in this city some half-dozen years ago. I used to write regularly for that paper, as you may remember."

"Oh yes, indeed !" I exclaimed. "And I shall never forget your 'Conundrum of the Anvil' which appeared in it. How often have I laughed at that most wonderful conceit, and how often have I put it to my friends ! "

Barbel gazed at me silently for a moment, and then he pointed to the frame. "That printed page," he said solemnly, "contains the 'Conundrum of the Anvil.' I hang it there, so that I can see it while I work.

That conundrum ruined me.   It was the last thing I wrote for *The Grasshopper*.   How I ever came to imagine it, I cannot tell.   It is one of those things which occur to a man but once in a lifetime.   After the wild shout of delight with which the public greeted that conundrum, my subsequent efforts met with hoots of derision.   *The Grasshopper* turned its hind-legs upon me.   I sank from bad to worse,—much worse, until at last I found myself reduced to my present occupation, which is that of grinding points to pins.   By this I procure my bread, coffee, and tobacco, and sometimes potatoes and meat.   One day while I was hard at work, an organ-grinder came into the street below.   He played the serenade from 'Trovatore;' and the familiar notes brought back visions of old days and old delights, when the successful writer wore good clothes and sat at operas, when he looked into sweet eyes and talked of Italian airs, when his future appeared all a succession of bright scenery and joyous acts, without any provision for a drop-curtain.   And as my ear listened, and my mind wandered in this happy retrospect, my every faculty seemed exalted, and, without any thought upon the matter, I ground points upon my pins so fine, so regular and smooth, that they would have pierced with ease the leather of a boot, or slipped among, without abrasion, the finest threads of rare old lace. When the organ stopped, and I fell back into my real world of cobwebs and mustiness, I gazed upon the pins I had just ground, and, without a moment's hesitation, I threw them into the street, and reported the lot as spoiled. This cost me a little money, but it saved me my livelihood."

After a few moments of silence, Barbel resumed—

"I have no more to say to you, my young friend. All I want you to do is to look upon that framed conundrum, then upon this grindstone, and then to go home and reflect. As for me, I have a gross of pins to grind before the sun goes down."

I cannot say that my depression of mind was at all relieved by what I had seen and heard. I had lost sight of Barbel for some years, and I had.supposed him still floating on the sun-sparkling stream of prosperity where I had last seen him. It was a great shock to me to find him in such a condition of poverty and squalor, and to see a man who had originated the "Conundrum of the Anvil" reduced to the soul-depressing occupation of grinding pin-points. As I walked and thought, the dreadful picture of a totally eclipsed future arose before my mind. The moral of Barbel sank deep into my heart.

When I reached home I told my wife the story of my friend Barbel. She listened with a sad and eager interest.

"I am afraid," she said, "if our fortunes do not quickly mend, that we shall have to buy two little grindstones. You know I could help you at that sort of thing."

For a long time we sat together and talked, and devised many plans for the future. I did not think it necessary yet for me to look out for a pin-contract; but I must find some way of making money, or we should starve to death. Of course, the first thing that suggested itself was the possibility of finding some other business; but, apart from the difficulty of immediately obtaining remunerative work in occupations to which I had not been trained, I felt a great and natural reluctance to give up a profession for which I had carefully prepared myself, and which I had adopted as my life-work. It would be very hard for me to lay down my pen for ever, and to close the top of my inkstand upon all the bright and happy fancies which I had seen mirrored in its tranquil pool. We talked and pondered the rest of that day and a good deal of the night, but we came to no conclusion as to what it would be best for us to do.

The next day I determined to go and call upon the editor of the journal for which, in happier days, before the blight of "His Wife's Deceased Sister" rested upon me, I used most frequently to write, and, having frankly explained my condition to him, to ask his advice. The editor was a good man, and had always been my friend. He listened with great attention to what I told him, and evidently sympathised with me in my trouble.

"As we have written to you," he said, "the only reason why we did not accept the manuscripts you sent us was, that they would have disappointed the high hopes that the public had formed in regard to you. We have had letter after letter asking when we were going to publish another story like 'His Wife's Deceased Sister.'- We felt, and we still feel, that it would be wrong to allow you to destroy the fair fabric which yourself has raised. But," he added, with a kind smile, "I see very plainly that your well-deserved reputation will be of little advantage to you if you should starve at the moment that its genial beams are, so to speak, lighting you up."

"Its beams are not genial," I answered. "They have scorched and withered me."

"How would you like," said the editor, after a short reflection, "to allow us to publish the stories you have recently written under some other name than your own? That would satisfy us and the public, would put money in your pocket, and would not interfere with your reputation."

Joyfully I seized that noble fellow by the hand, and instantly accepted his proposition. "Of course," said I, "a reputation is a very good thing; but no reputation can take the place of food, clothes, and a house to live in; and I gladly agree to sink my over-illumined name-into oblivion, and to appear before the public as a new and unknown writer."

"I hope that need not be for long," he said, "for I feel sure that you will yet write stories as good as 'His Wife's Deceased Sister.'"

All the manuscripts I had on hand I now sent to my good friend the editor, and in due and proper order they appeared in his journal under the name of John Darmstadt, which I had selected as a substitute for my own, permanently disabled. I made a similar arrangement with other editors, and John Darmstadt received the credit of everything that proceeded from my pen. Our circumstances now became very comfortable, and occasionally we even allowed ourselves to indulge in little dreams of prosperity.

Time passed on very pleasantly ; one year, another, and then a little son was born to us. It is often difficult, I believe, for thoughtful persons to decide whether the beginning of their conjugal career, or the earliest weeks in the life of their first-born, be the happiest and proudest period of their existence. For myself I can only say that the same exaltation of mind, the same rarefication of idea and invention, which succeeded upon my wedding-day came upon me now. As then my ecstatic emotions crystallised themselves into a motive for a story, and without delay I set myself to work upon it. My boy was about six weeks old when the manuscript was finished ; and one evening, as we sat before a comfortable fire in our sitting-room, with the curtains drawn, and the soft lamp lighted, and the baby sleeping soundly in the adjoining chamber, I read the story to my wife.

When I had finished, my wife arose, and threw herself into my arms. "I was never so proud of you," she said, her glad eyes sparkling, "as I am at this moment. That is a wonderful story! It is, indeed I am sure it is, just as good as 'His Wife's Deceased Sister.'"

As she spoke these words, a sudden and chilling sensation crept over us both. All her warmth and fervour, and the proud and happy glow engendered within me by this praise and appreciation from one I loved, vanished in an instant. We stepped apart, and gazed upon each other with pallid faces. In the same moment the terrible truth had flashed upon us both.

This story *was* as good as "His Wife's Deceased Sister"!

We stood silent. The exceptional lot of Barbél's super-pointed pins seemed to pierce our very souls. A dreadful vision rose before me of an impending fall and crash, in which our domestic happiness should vanish, and our prospects for our boy be wrecked, just as we had begun to build them up.

My wife approached me, and took my hand in hers, which was as cold as ice. "Be strong and firm," she said. "A great danger threatens us, but you must brace yourself against it. Be strong and firm."

I pressed her hand, and we said no more that night.

The next day I took the manuscript I had

just written, and carefully enfolded it in stout wrapping-paper. Then I went to a neighbouring grocery store, and bought a small, strong, tin box, originally intended for biscuit, with a cover that fitted tightly. In this I placed my manuscript; and then I took the box to a tinsmith, and had the top fastened on with hard solder. When I went home I ascended into the garret, and brought down to my study a ship's cash-box, which had once belonged to one of my family who was a sea-captain. This box was very heavy, and firmly bound with iron, and was secured by two massive locks. Calling my wife, I told her of the contents of the tin case, which I then placed in the box, and, having shut down the heavy lid, I doubly locked it.

"This key," said I, putting it in my pocket, "I shall throw into the river when I go out this afternoon."

My wife watched me eagerly, with a pallid and firm, set countenance, but upon which I could see the faint glimmer of returning happiness.

"Wouldn't it be well," she said, "to secure it still further by sealing-wax and pieces of tape?"

"No," said I. "I do not believe that any one will attempt to tamper with our prosperity. And now, my dear," I continued in an impressive voice, "no one but you, and, in the course of time, our son, shall know that this manuscript exists. When I am dead, those who survive me may, if they see fit, cause this box to be split open, and the story published. The reputation it may give my name cannot harm me then."

THE REMARKABLE WRECK OF
THE "THOMAS HYKE."

THE REMARKABLE WRECK OF THE "THOMAS HYKE."

IT was half-past one by the clock in the office of the Registrar of Woes. The room was empty, for it was Wednesday, and the Registrar always went home early on Wednesday afternoons. He had made that arrangement when he accepted the office. He was willing to serve his fellow-citizens in any suitable position to which he might be called, but he had private interests which could not be neglected. He belonged to his country, but there was a house in the country which belonged to him; and there were a great many things appertaining to that house which needed attention, especially in pleasant summer weather. It is true he was often absent on afternoons which did not fall on the Wednesday, but the fact of his having appointed a particular time for the furtherance of his outside interests so emphasised their importance that his associates in the office had no difficulty in understanding that affairs of such moment could not always be attended to in a single afternoon of the week.

But although the large room devoted to the especial use of the Registrar was unoccupied, there were other rooms connected with it which were not in that condition. With the suite of offices to the left we have nothing to do, but will confine our attention to a moderate-sized room to the right of the Registrar's office, and connected by a door, now closed, with that large and handsomely furnished chamber. This was the office of the Clerk of Shipwrecks, and it was at present occupied by five persons. One of these was the clerk himself, a man of goodly appearance, somewhere between twenty-five and forty-five years of age, and of a demeanour such as might be supposed to belong to one who had occupied a high position in State affairs, but who, by the cabals of his enemies, had been forced to resign the great operations of statesmanship which he had been directing, and who now stood, with a quite resigned air, pointing out to the populace the futile and disastrous efforts of the incompetent one who was endeavouring to fill his place. The Clerk of Shipwrecks had never fallen from such a position, having never occupied one, but he had acquired the demeanour referred to without going through the preliminary exercises.

Another occupant was a very young man, the personal clerk of the Registrar of Woes, who always closed all the doors of the office of that functionary on Wednesday afternoons, and at other times when outside interest demanded his principal's absence, after which he betook himself to the room of his friend the Shipwreck Clerk.

Then there was a middle-aged man named Matthers, also a friend of the clerk, and who was one of the eight who had made application for a sub-position in this department, which was now filled by a man who was expected to resign when a friend of his, a gentleman of influence in an interior county, should succeed in procuring the nomination as congressional representative of his district of an influential politician, whose election was considered assured in case certain expected action on the part of the administration should bring his party into power. The person now occupying the sub-position hoped to get something better, and Matthers, consequently, was very willing, while waiting for the place, to visit the offices of the department and acquaint himself with its duties.

A fourth person was J. George Watts, a juryman by profession, who had brought with him his brother-in-law, a stranger in the city.

The Shipwreck Clerk had taken off his good coat, which he had worn to luncheon, and had replaced it by a lighter garment of linen, much bespattered with ink; and he now produced a cigar-box, containing six cigars.

"Gents," said he, "here is the fag end of a box of cigars. It's not like having the pick of the box, but they are all I have left."

Mr. Matthers, J. George Watts, and the brother-in-law each took a cigar with that careless yet deferential manner which always distinguishes the treatee from the treator; and then the box was protruded in an off-hand way toward Harry Covare, the personal clerk of the Registrar; but this young man declined, saying that he preferred cigarettes, a package of which he drew from his pocket. He had very often seen that cigar-box with a Havana brand, which he himself had brought from the other room after the Registrar had emptied it, passed around with six cigars, no more nor less, and he was wise enough to know that the Shipwreck Clerk did not expect to supply him with smoking material. If that gentleman had offered to the friends who generally dropped in on him on Wednesday afternoon the paper bag of cigars sold at five cents each when bought singly, but half a dozen for a quarter of a dollar, they would have been quite as thankfully received ; but it better pleased his deprecative soul to put them in an empty cigar-box, and thus throw around them the halo of the presumption that ninety-four of their imported companions had been smoked.

The Shipwreck Clerk, having lighted a cigar for himself, sat down in his revolving chair, turned his back to his desk, and threw himself into an easy cross-legged attitude, which showed that he was perfectly at home in that office. Harry Covare mounted a high stool, while the visitors seated themselves in three wooden arm-chairs. But few words had been said, and each man had scarcely tossed his first tobacco ashes on the floor, when some one wearing heavy boots was heard opening an outside door and entering the Registrar's room. Harry Covare jumped down from his stool, laid his half-smoked cigarette thereon, and bounced into the next room, closing the door after him. In about a minute he returned, and the Shipwreck Clerk looked at him inquiringly.

"An old cock in a pea-jacket," said Mr. Covare, taking up his cigarette, and mounting his stool. "I told him the Registrar would be here in the morning. He said he had something to report about a shipwreck ; and I told him the Registrar would be here in the morning. Had to tell him that three times, and then he went."

"School don't keep Wednesday afternoons," said Mr. J. George Watts with a knowing smile.

"No, sir," said the Shipwreck Clerk, emphatically, changing the crossing of his legs. "A man can't keep grinding on day in and out without breaking down. Outsiders may say what they please about it, but it can't be done. We 've got to let up sometimes. People who do the work need the rest just as much as those who do the looking on."

"And more, too, I should say," observed Mr. Matthers.

"Our little let-up on Wednesday afternoons," modestly observed Harry Covare, "is like death; it is sure to come, while the let-ups we get other days are more like the diseases which prevail in certain areas; you can't be sure whether you're going to get them or not."

The Shipwreck Clerk smiled benignantly at this remark, and the rest laughed. Mr. Matthers had heard it before, but he would not impair the pleasantness of his relations with a future colleague by hinting that he remembered it.

"He gets such ideas from his beastly statistics," said the Shipwreck Clerk.

"Which come pretty heavy on him sometimes, I expect," observed Mr. Matthers.

"They needn't," said the Shipwreck Clerk, "if things were managed here as they ought to be. If John J. Laylor," meaning thereby the Registrar, "was the right kind of a man, you'd see things very different here from what they are now. There'd be a larger force."

"That's so," said Mr. Matthers.

"And not only that, but there'd be better buildings, and more accommodations. Were any of you ever up to Anster? Well, take a run up there some day, and see what sort of buildings the department has there. William Q. Green is a very different man from John

J. Laylor.   You don't see him sitting in his chair and picking his teeth the whole winter, while the representative from his district never says a word about his department from one end of a session of Congress to the other. Now if I had charge of things here, I 'd make such changes that you wouldn't know the place.   I 'd throw two rooms off here, and a corridor and entrance door at that end of the building.   I 'd close up this door," pointing toward the Registrar's room, "and if John J. Laylor wanted to come in here, he might go round to the end door like other people."

The thought struck Harry Covare that in that case there would be no John J. Laylor, but he would not interrupt.

"And what is more," continued the Shipwreck Clerk, "I 'd close up this whole department at twelve o'clock on Saturdays. The way things are managed now, a man has no time to attend to his own private business. Suppose I think of buying a piece of land, and want to go out and look at it; or suppose any one of you gentlemen were here, and thought of buying a piece of land and wanted to go out and look at it, what are you going to do about it? You don't want to go on Sunday, and when are you going to go?"

Not one of the other gentlemen had ever

thought of buying a piece of land, nor had they any reason to suppose that they ever would purchase an inch of soil unless they bought it in a flower-pot ; but they all agreed that the way things were managed now, there was no time for a man to attend to his own business.

"But you can't expect John J. Laylor to do anything," said the Shipwreck Clerk.

However, there was one thing which that gentleman always expected John J. Laylor to do. When the Clerk was surrounded by a number of persons in hours of business, and when he had succeeded in impressing them with the importance of his functions, and the necessity of paying deferential attention to himself if they wished their business attended to, John J. Laylor would be sure to walk into the office and address the Shipwreck Clerk in such a manner as to let the people present know that he was a clerk and nothing else, and that he, the Registrar, was the head of that department. These humiliations the Shipwreck Clerk never forgot.

There was a little pause here, and then Mr. Matthers remarked—

"I should think you 'd be awful bored with the long stories of shipwrecks that the people come and tell you."

He hoped to change the conversation, because, although he wished to remain on good terms with the subordinate officers, it was not desirable that he should be led to say much against John J. Laylor.

"No, sir," said the Shipwreck Clerk, "I am not bored. I did not come here to be bored, and as long as I have charge of this office I don't intend to be. The long-winded old salts who come here to report their wrecks never spin out their prosy yarns to me. The first thing I do is to let them know just what I want of them; and not an inch beyond that does a man of them go, at least while I am managing the business. There are times when John J. Laylor comes in, and puts in his oar, and wants to hear the whole story, which is pure stuff and nonsense, for John J. Laylor doesn't know anything more about a shipwreck than he does about——"

"The endemics in the Lake George area," suggested Harry Covare.

"Yes; or any other part of his business," said the Shipwreck Clerk; "and when he takes it into his head to interfere, all business stops till some second mate of a coal-schooner has told his whole story, from his sighting land on the morning of one day to his getting ashore on it on the afternoon of the next.——

Now I don't put up with any such nonsense.
There's no man living that can tell me anything about shipwrecks.   I've never been to
sea myself, but that's not necessary ; and if
I had gone, it's not likely I'd been wrecked.
But I've read about every kind of shipwreck
that ever happened.   When I first came
here I took care to post myself upon these
matters, because I knew it would. save
trouble.   I have read *Robinson Crusoe*,
' The Wreck of the *Grosvenor*,' ' The Sinking
of the *Royal George*,' and wrecks by water-
spouts, tidal waves, and every other thing
which would knock a ship into a cocked hat,
and I've classified every sort of wreck under
its proper head ; and when I've found out to
what class a wreck belongs, I know all about
it.   Now, when a man comes here to report
a wreck, the first thing he has to do is just
to shut down on his story, and to stand up
square and answer a few questions that I put
to him.   In two minutes I know just what
kind of shipwreck he's had ; and then, when
he gives me the name of his vessel, and one
or two other points, he may go.   I know all
about that wreck, and I make a much better
report of the business than he could have
done if he'd stood here talking three days
and three nights. The amount of money

that's been saved to our tax-payers by the way I've systematised the business of this office is not to be calculated in figures."

The brother-in-law of J. George Watts knocked the ashes from the remnant of his cigar, looked contemplatively at the coal for a moment, and then remarked—

"I think you said there's no kind of ship-wreck you don't know about?"

"That's what I said," replied the Ship-wreck Clerk.

"I think," said the other, "I could tell you of a shipwreck, in which I was concerned, that wouldn't go into any of your classes."

The Shipwreck Clerk threw away the end of his cigar, put both his hands into his trousers pockets, stretched out his legs, and looked steadfastly at the man who had made this unwarrantable remark. Then a pitying smile stole over his countenance, and he said: "Well, sir, I'd like to hear your account of it; and before you get a quarter through I can stop you just where you are, and go ahead and tell the rest of the story my-self."

"That's so," said Harry Covare. "You'll see him do it just as sure pop as a spread rail bounces the engine."

"Well, then," said the brother-in-law of

J. George Watts, "I'll tell it."   And he began :—

"It was just two years ago, the first of this month, that I sailed for South America in the *Thomas Hyke.*"

At this point the Shipwreck Clerk turned and opened a large book at the letter T.

"That wreck wasn't reported here," said the other, "and you won't find it in your book."

"At Anster, perhaps?" said the Shipwreck Clerk, closing the volume, and turning round again.

"Can't say about that," replied the other. "I've never been to Anster, and haven't looked over their books."

"Well, you needn't want to," said the clerk.   "They've got good accommodations at Anster, and the Registrar has some ideas of the duties of his post, but they have no such system of wreck reports as we have here."

"Very like," said the brother-in-law.   And he went on with his story.   "The *Thomas Hyke* was a small iron steamer of six hundred tons, and she sailed from Ulford for Valparaiso with a cargo principally of pig-iron."

" Pig-iron for Valparaiso ? " remarked the Shipwreck Clerk.   And then he knitted his brows thoughtfully, and said, " Go on."

" She was a new vessel," continued the narrator, " and built with water-tight compartments ; rather uncommon for a vessel of her class, but so she was. I am not a sailor, and don't know anything about ships. I went as passenger, and there was another one named William Anderson, and his son Sam, a boy about fifteen years old. We were all going to Valparaiso on business. I don't remember just how many days we were out, nor do I know just where we were, but it was somewhere off the coast of South America, when, one dark night, with a fog besides, for aught I know, for I was asleep, we ran into a steamer coming north. How we managed to do this, with room enough on both sides for all the ships in the world to pass, I don't know ; but so it was. When I got on deck the other vessel had gone on, and we never saw anything more of her. Whether she sunk or got home is something I can't tell. But we pretty soon found that the *Thomas Hyke* had some of the plates in her bow badly smashed, and she took in water like a thirsty dog. The captain had the forward water-tight bulkhead shut tight, and the pumps set to work, but it was no use. That forward compartment just filled up with water, and the *Thomas Hyke* settled down with her bow clean under. Her deck was slanting forward like the side of a hill, and the propeller was lifted up so that it wouldn't have worked even if the engine had been kept going. The captain had the masts cut away, thinking this might bring her up some, but it didn't help much. There was a pretty heavy sea on, and the waves came rolling up the slant of the deck like the surf on the sea-shore. The captain gave orders to have all the hatches battened down, so that water couldn't get in, and the only way by which anybody could go below was by the cabin-door, which was far aft. This work of stopping up all openings in the deck was a dangerous business, for the decks sloped right down into the water, and if anybody had slipped, away he 'd have gone into the ocean, with nothing to stop him ; but the men made a line fast to themselves, and worked away with a good will, and soon got the deck and the house over the engine as tight as a bottle. The smoke-stack, which was well forward, had been broken down by a spar when the masts had been cut, and as the waves washed into the hole that it left, the captain had this plugged up with old sails, well fastened down. It was a dreadful thing to see the ship a-lying with her bows clean under water, and her stern sticking up.   If it hadn't been for her water-tight compartments that were left uninjured, she would have gone down to the bottom as slick as a whistle.   On the afternoon of the day after the collision the wind fell, and the sea soon became pretty smooth. The captain was quite sure that there would be no trouble about keeping afloat until some ship came along and took us off.   Our flag was flying, upside down, from a pole in the stern ; and if anybody saw a ship making such a guy of herself as the *Thomas Hyke* was then doing, they'd be sure to come to see what was the matter with her, even if she had no flag of distress flying.   We tried to make ourselves as comfortable as we could, but this wasn't easy with everything on such a dreadful slant.   But that night we heard a rumbling and grinding noise down in the hold, and the slant seemed to get worse. Pretty soon the captain roused all hands, and told us that the cargo of pig-iron was shifting, and sliding down to the bow, and that it wouldn't be long before it would break through all the bulkheads, and then we'd fill and go to the bottom like a shot.

He said we must all take to the boats, and
get away as quick as we could. It was an
easy matter launching the boats. They
didn't lower them outside from the davits,
but they just let 'em down on deck, and slid
'em along forward into the water, and then
held 'em there with a rope till everything
was ready to start. They launched three
boats, put plenty of provisions and water in
'em, and then everybody began to get aboard.
But William Anderson, and me, and his son
Sam, couldn't make up our minds to get into
those boats and row out on the dark, wide
ocean. They were the biggest boats we had,
but still they were little things enough. The
ship seemed to us to be a good deal safer,
and more likely to be seen when day broke,
than those three boats, which might be
blown off if the wind rose, nobody knew
where. It seemed to us that the cargo had
done all the shifting it intended to, for the
noise below had stopped ; and, altogether,
we agreed that we 'd rather stick to the ship
than go off in those boats. The captain, he
tried to make us go, but we wouldn't do it ;
and he told us if we chose to stay behind and
be drowned it was our affair, and he couldn't
help it ; and then he said there was a small
boat aft, and we 'd better launch her, and

have her ready in case things should get worse, and we should make up our minds to leave the vessel. He and the rest then rowed off so as not to be caught in the vortex if the steamer went down, and we three stayed aboard. We launched the small boat in the way we 'd seen the others launched, being careful to have ropes tied to us while we were doing it; and we put things aboard that we thought we should want. Then we went into the cabin, and waited for morning. It was a queer kind of a cabin, with a floor inclined like the roof of a house, but we sat down in the corners, and were glad to be there. The swinging lamp was burning, and it was a good deal more cheerful in there than it was outside. But, about daybreak, the grinding and rumbling down below began again, and the bow of the *Thomas Hyke* kept going down more and more; and it wasn't long before the forward bulkhead of the cabin, which was what you might call its front wall when everything was all right, was under our feet, as level as a floor, and the lamp was lying close against the ceiling that it was hanging from. You may be sure that we thought it was time to get out of that. There were benches with arms to them fastened to the floor, and by these we climbed

up to the foot of the cabin stairs, which,
being turned bottom upward, we went down
in order to get out.   When we reached the
cabin door we saw part of the deck below
us standing up like the side of a house that
is built in the water, as they say the houses
in Venice are.   We had made our boat fast
to the cabin door by a long line, and now we
saw her floating quietly on the water, which
was very smooth, and about twenty feet below us.   We drew her up as close under us as
we could, and then we let the boy Sam down
by a rope, and, after some kicking and
swinging, he got into her ; and then he took
the oars, and kept her right under us while
we scrambled down by the ropes which we
had used in getting her ready.   As soon as
we were in the boat we cut her rope and
pulled away as hard as we could ; and when
we got to what we thought was a safe distance we stopped to look at the *Thomas
Hyke*.   You never saw such a ship in all your
born days.   Two-thirds of the hull was sunk
in the water, and she was standing straight
up and down, with the stern in the air, her
rudder up as high as the topsail ought to be,
and the screw-propeller looking like the
wheel on the top of one of these windmills
that they have in the country for pumping

up water.   Her cargo had shifted so far forward that it had turned her right up on end, but she couldn't sink, owing to the air in the compartments that the water hadn't got into; and on the top of the whole thing was the distress flag flying from the pole which stuck out over the stern.   It was broad daylight, but not a thing did we see of the other boats.   We'd supposed that they wouldn't row very far, but would lay off at a safe distance until daylight; but they must have been scared, and rowed further than they intended.   Well, sir, we stayed in that boat all day, and watched the *Thomas Hyke*, but she just kept as she was, and didn't seem to sink an inch.   There was no use of rowing away, for we had no place to row to; and besides, we thought that passing ships would be much more likely to see that stern sticking high in the air than our little boat.   We had enough to eat, and at night two of us slept while the other watched, dividing off the time, and taking turns to this.   In the morning there was the *Thomas Hyke* standing stern up just as before.   There was a long swell on the ocean now, and she'd rise and lean over a little on each wave, but she'd come up again just as straight as before.   That night passed as the last one had, and in the morning we found we'd drifted a good deal further from the *Thomas Hyke*, but she was floating just as she had been, like a big buoy that's moored over a sand-bar.   We couldn't see a sign of the boats, and we about gave them up.   We had our breakfast, which was a pretty poor meal, being nothing but hard-tack and what was left of a piece of boiled beef.   After we'd sat for a while doing nothing, but feeling mighty uncomfortable, William Anderson said : 'Look here, do you know that I think we would be three fools to keep on shivering all night and living on hard-tack in the day-time, when there's plenty on that vessel for us to eat, and to keep us warm.   If she's floated that way for two days and two nights, there's no knowing how much longer she'll float, and we might as well go on board and get the things we want as not.'   'All right,' said I, for I was tired doing nothing, and Sam was as willing as anybody.   So we rowed up to the steamer, and stopped close to the deck, which, as I said before, was standing straight up out of the water like the wall of a house.   The cabin door, which was the only opening into her, was about twenty feet above us, and the ropes which we had tied to the rails of the stairs inside were still hanging down. Sam was an active youngster, and he managed to climb up one of these ropes ; but when he got to the door he drew it up and tied knots in it about a foot apart, and then he let it down to us, for neither William Anderson nor me could go up a rope hand over hand without knots or something to hold on to. As it was, we had a lot of bother getting up, but we did it at last, and then we walked up the stairs, treading on the front part of each step instead of the top of it, as we would have done if the stairs had been in their proper position. When we got to the floor of the cabin, which was now perpendicular like a wall, we had to clamber down by means of the furniture, which was screwed fast, until we reached the bulkhead, which was now the floor of the cabin. Close to this bulkhead was a small room which was the steward's pantry, and here we found lots of things to eat, but all jumbled up in a way that made us laugh. The boxes of biscuits and the tin cans, and a lot of bottles in wicker covers, were piled up on one end of the room, and everything in the lockers and drawers was jumbled together. William Anderson and me set to work to get out what we thought we'd want, and we told Sam to climb up

into some of the state-rooms, of which there
were four on each side of the cabin, and get
some blankets to keep us warm, as well as a
few sheets, which we thought we could rig
up for an awning to the boat; for the days
were just as hot as the nights were cool.
When we'd collected what we wanted,
William Anderson and me climbed into our
own rooms, thinking we'd each pack a valise
with what we most wanted to save of our
clothes and things; and while we were doing
this, Sam called out to us that it was raining.
He was sitting at the cabin door looking out.
I first thought to tell him to shut the door
so's to keep the rain from coming in; but
when I thought how things really were, I
laughed at the idea. There was a sort of
little house built over the entrance to the
cabin, and in one end of it was the door;
and in the way the ship now was the open
doorway was underneath the little house,
and of course no rain could come in. Pretty
soon we heard the rain pouring down, beating on the stern of the vessel like hail. We
got to the stairs and looked out. The rain
was falling in perfect sheets, in a way you
never see except round about the tropics.
'It's a good thing we're inside,' said William Anderson, 'for if we'd been out in this

rain we'd been drowned in the boat.'   I agreed with him, and we made up our minds to stay where we were until the rain was over. Well, it rained about four hours; and when it stopped, and we looked out, we saw our little boat nearly full of water, and sunk so deep that if one of us had stepped on her she'd have gone down, sure. 'Here's a pretty kittle of fish,' said William Anderson; 'there's nothing for us to do now but to stay where we are.' I believe in his heart he was glad of that, for if ever a man was tired of a little boat, William Anderson was tired of that one we'd been in for two days and two nights. At any rate there was no use talking about it, and we set to work to make ourselves comfortable. We got some mattresses and pillows out of the state-rooms, and when it began to get dark we lighted the lamp, which we had filled with sweet-oil from a flask in the pantry, not finding any other kind, and we hung it from the railing of the stairs. We had a good night's rest, and the only thing that disturbed me was William Anderson lifting up his head every time he turned over, and saying how much better this was than that blasted little boat. The next morning we had a good breakfast, even mak-

ing some tea with a spirit lamp we found,
using brandy instead of alcohol. William
Anderson and I wanted to get into the captain's room, which was near the stern, and
pretty high up, so as to see if there was anything there that we ought to get ready to
save when a vessel should come along and
pick us up; but we were not good at climb-
ing, like Sam, and we didn't see how we
could get up there. Sam said he was sure
he had once seen a ladder in the compartment just forward of the bulkhead, and as
William was very anxious to get up to the
captain's room, we let the boy go and look
for it. There was a sliding door in the bulkhead under our feet, and we opened this far
enough to let Sam get through; and he
scrambled down like a monkey into the next
compartment, which was light enough, although the lower half of it, which was next
to the engine-room, was under the water-
line. Sam actually found a ladder, with
hooks at one end of it, and while he was
handing it up to us, which was very hard to
do, for he had to climb up on all sorts of
things, he let it topple over, and the end
with the iron hooks fell against the round
glass of one of the port-holes. The glass
was very thick and strong, but the ladder

came down very heavy and shivered it.   As bad luck would have it, this window was below the water-line, and the water came rushing in in a big spout. We chucked blankets down to Sam for him to stop up the hole, but 'twas of no use; for it was hard for him to get at the window, and when he did the water came in with such force that he couldn't get a blanket into the hole.   We were afraid he'd be drowned down there, and told him to come out as quick as he could. He put up the ladder again, and hooked it on to the door in the bulkhead, and we held it while he climbed up.   Looking down through the doorway, we saw, by the way the water was pouring in at the opening, that it wouldn't be long before that compartment was filled up; so we shoved the door to and made it all tight, and then said William Anderson: 'The ship'll sink deeper and deeper as that fills up, and the water may get up to the cabin door, and we must go and make that as tight as we can.' Sam had pulled the ladder up after him, and this we found of great use in getting to the foot of the cabin stairs. We shut the cabin door, and locked and bolted it; and as it fitted pretty tight, we didn't think it would let in much water if the ship sank that far.

But over the top of the cabin stairs were a couple of folding doors, which shut down horizontally when the ship was in its proper position, and which were only used in very bad, cold weather. These we pulled to and fastened tight, thus having a double protection against the water, Well, we didn't get this done any too soon, for the water did come up to the cabin door, and a little trickled in from the outside door, and through the cracks in the inner one. But we went to work and stopped these up with strips from the sheets, which we crammed well in with our pocket knives. Then we sat down on the steps, and waited to see what would happen next. The doors of all the state-rooms were open, and we could see through the thick plate-glass windows in them, which were all shut tight, that the ship was sinking more and more as the water came in. Sam climbed up into one of the after state-rooms, and said the outside water was nearly up to the stern ; and pretty soon we looked up to the two port-holes in the stern, and saw that they were covered with water ; and as more and more water could be seen there, and as the light came through less easily, we knew that we were sinking . under the surface of the ocean. ' It's a

mighty good thing,' said William Anderson,
'that no water can get in here.' William
had a hopeful kind of mind, and always
looked on the bright side of things ; but I
must say that I was dreadfully scared when
I looked through those stern windows and
saw water instead of sky. It began to get
duskier and duskier as we sank lower and
lower ; but still we could see pretty well, for
it 's astonishing how much light comes down
through water. After a little while we
noticed that the light remained about the
same ; and then William Anderson he sings
out : 'Hooray, we 've stopped sinking !'
'What difference does that make ?' says I.
'We must be thirty or forty feet under
water, and more yet for aught I know.'
'Yes, that may be,' said he ; 'but it is
clear' that all the water has got into that
compartment that can get in, and we have
sunk just as far down as we are going.'
'But that don't help matters,' said I ;
'thirty or forty feet under water is just as
bad as a thousand as to drowning a man.'
'Drowning !' said William ; 'how are you
going to be drowned? No water can get in
here.'   'Nor no air either,' said I ; 'and
. people are drowned for want of air, as I take
it.'   'It would be a queer sort of thing,'

said William, 'to be drowned in the ocean and yet stay as dry as a chip. But it's no use being worried about air. We've got air enough here to last us for ever so long. This stern compartment is the biggest in the ship, and it's got lots of air in it. Just think of that hold ; it must be nearly full of air. The stern compartment of the hold has got nothing in it but sewing-machines. I saw 'em loading her. The pig-iron was mostly amidships, or at least forward of this compartment. Now, there's no kind of a cargo that'll accommodate as much air as sewing-machines. They're packed in wooden frames, not boxes, and don't fill up half the room they take. There's air all through and around 'em. It's a very comforting thing to think the hold isn't filled up solid with bales of cotton or wheat in bulk.' It might be comforting, but I couldn't get much good out of it. And now Sam, who'd been scrambling all over the cabin to see how things were going on, sang out that the water was leaking in a little again at the cabin door, and around some of the iron frames of the windows. 'It's a lucky thing,' said William Anderson, 'that we didn't sink any deeper, or the pressure of the water would have burst in those heavy glasses. And what we 've got to do now is to stop up all the cracks. The more we work, the livelier we 'll feel.' We tore off more strips of sheets, and went all round stopping up cracks wherever we found them. 'It 's fortunate,' said William Anderson, 'that Sam found that ladder, for we would have had hard work getting to the windows of the stern state-rooms without it ; but by resting it on the bottom step of the stairs, which now happens to be the top one, we can get to any part of the cabin.' I couldn't help thinking that if Sam hadn't found the ladder it would have been a good deal better for us ; but I didn't want to damp William's spirits, and I said nothing.

"And now I beg your pardon, sir," said the narrator, addressing the Shipwreck Clerk, "but I forgot that you said you 'd finish this story yourself. Perhaps you 'd like to take it up just here ?"

The Shipwreck Clerk seemed surprised, and had, apparently, forgotten his previous offer. "Oh no," said he, "tell your own story. This is not a matter of business."

"Very well, then," said the brother-in-law of J. George Watts, "I 'll go on. We made everything as tight as we could, and then we got our supper, having forgotten all about dinner, and being very hungry. We didn't make any tea, and we didn't light the lamp, for we knew that would use up air; but we made a better meal than three people sunk out of sight in the ocean had a right to expect. 'What troubles me most,' said William Anderson, as he turned in, 'is the fact that if we are forty feet under water, our flág-pole must be covered up. Now, if the flag was sticking out, upside down, a ship sailing by would see it, and would know there was something wrong.' 'If that's all that troubles you,' said I, 'I guess you'll sleep easy. And if a ship was to see the flag, I wonder how they'd know we were down here, and how they'd get us out if they did!' 'Oh, they'd manage it,' said William Anderson; 'trust those sea-captains for that.' And then he went to sleep. The next morning the air began to get mighty disagreeable in the part of the cabin where we were, and then William Anderson he says: 'What we've got to do is to climb up into the stern state-rooms, where the air is purer. We can come down here to get our meals, and then go up again to breathe comfortable.' 'And what are we going to do when the air up there gets foul?' says I to William, who seemed to be making arrangements for spending the summer in our present quarters. 'Oh, that'll be all right,' said he. 'It don't do to be extravagant with air any more than with anything else. When we've used up all there is in this cabin, we can bore holes through the floor into the hold and let in air from there. If we're economical, there'll be enough to last for dear knows how long.' We passed the night each in a state-room, sleeping on the end wall instead of the berth, and it wasn't till the afternoon of the next day that the air of the cabin got so bad we thought we'd have some fresh; so we went down on the bulkhead, and with an auger that we found in the pantry we bored three holes, about a yard apart, in the cabin floor, which was now one of the walls of the room, just as the bulkhead was the floor, and the stern end, where the two round windows were, was the ceiling or roof. We each took a hole, and I tell you it was pleasant to breathe the air which came in from the hold. 'Isn't this jolly?' said William Anderson. 'And we ought to be mighty glad that that hold wasn't loaded with cod-fish or soap. But there's nothing that smells better than new sewing-machines that haven't ever been used, and this air is pleasant enough for anybody.' By William's advice we made three plugs, by which we stopped up the holes when we thought we 'd had air enough for the present. 'And now,' says he, 'we needn't climb up into those awkward state-rooms any more. We can just stay down here and be comfortable, and let in air when we want it.' 'And how long do you suppose that air in the hold is going to last?' said I. 'Oh, ever so long,' said he, 'using it so economically as we do ; and when it stops coming out lively through these little holes, as I suppose it will after a while, we can saw a big hole in this flooring and go into the hold, and do our breathing, if we want to.' That evening we did saw a hole about a foot square, so as to have plenty of air while we were asleep, but we didn't go into the hold, it being pretty well filled up with machines ; though the next day Sam and I sometimes stuck our heads in for a good sniff of air, though William Anderson was opposed to this, being of the opinion that we ought to put ourselves on short rations of breathing, so as to make the supply of air hold out as long as possible. 'But what 's the good,' said I to William, 'of trying to make the air hold out, if we 've got to be suffocated in this place after all ?'

'What's the good?' says he. 'Haven't you enough biscuits, and canned meats, and plenty of other things to eat, and a barrel of water in that room opposite the pantry, not to speak of wine and brandy if you want to cheer yourself up a bit, and haven't we good mattresses to sleep on, and why shouldn't we try to live and be comfortable as long as we can?' 'What I want,' said I, 'is to get out of this box. The idea of being shut up in here down under the water is more than I can stand. I 'd rather take my chances going up to the surface and swimming about till I found a piece of the wreck, or something to float on.' 'You needn't think of anything of that sort,' said William, 'for if we were to open a door or a window to get out, the water 'd rush in and drive us back and fill up this place in no time; and then the whole concern would go to the bottom. And what would you do if you did get to the top of the water? It 's not likely you 'd find anything there to get on, and if you did you wouldn't live very long floating about with nothing to eat. No, sir,' says he, 'what we 've got to do is to be content with the comforts we have around us, and something will turn up to get us out of this; you see if it don't.' There was no use talking against

William Anderson, and I didn't say any more about getting out. As for Sam, he spent his time at the windows of the state-rooms a-looking out. We could see a good way into the water, further than you would think, and we sometimes saw fishes, especially porpoises, swimming about, most likely try-ing to find out what a ship was doing hanging bows down under the water. What troubled Sam was that a sword-fish might come along and jab his sword through one of the windows. In that case, it would be all up, or rather down, with us. Every now and then he'd sing out, 'Here comes one!' and then, just as I'd give a jump, he'd say, 'No, it isn't; it's a porpoise.' I thought from the first, and I think now, that it would have been a great deal better for us if that boy hadn't been along. That night there was a good deal of motion to the ship, and she swung about and rose up and down more than she had done since we'd been left in her. 'There must be a big sea running on top,' said William Anderson, 'and if we were up there we'd be tossed about dread-ful. Now the motion down here is just as easy as a cradle, and, what's more, we can't be sunk very deep; for if we were, there wouldn't be any motion at all.' About noon the next day we felt a sudden tremble and shake run through the whole ship, and far down under us we heard a rumbling and grinding that nearly scared me out of my wits. I first thought we'd struck bottom, but William he said that couldn't be, for it was just as light in the cabin as it had been, and if we'd gone down it would have grown much darker, of course. The rumbling stopped after a little while, and then it seemed to grow lighter instead of darker; and Sam, who was looking up at the stern windows over our heads, he sang out, 'Sky!' And, sure enough, we could see the blue sky, as clear as 'daylight, through those windows! And then the ship, she turned herself on the slant, pretty much as she had been when her forward compartment first took in water, and we found ourselves standing on the cabin floor instead of the bulkhead. I was near one of the open state-rooms; and as I looked in, there was the sunlight coming through the wet glass in the window, and more cheerful than anything I ever saw before in this world. William Anderson he just made one jump, and, unscrewing one of the state-room windows, he jerked it open. We had thought the air inside was good enough to last some time longer; but when that window was open and the fresh air came rushing in, it was a different sort of thing, I can tell you. William put his head out, and looked up and down and all around. 'She's nearly all out of water!' he shouted, 'and we can open the cabin door.' Then we all three rushed at those stairs, which were nearly right side up now, and we had the cabin doors open in no time. When we looked out we saw that the ship was truly floating pretty much as she had been when the captain and crew left her, though we all agreed that her deck didn't slant as much forward as it did then. 'Do you know what's happened?' sang out William Anderson, after he'd stood still for a minute to look around and think. 'That bobbing up and down that the vessel got last night shook up and settled down the pig-iron inside of her, and the iron plates in the bow, that were smashed and loosened by the collision, have given way under the weight, and the whole cargo of pig-iron has burst through and gone to the bottom. Then, of course, up we came. 'Didn't I tell you something would happen to make us all right?'

"Well, I won't make this story any longer

than I can help. The next day after that we were taken off by a sugar-ship bound north, and we were carried safe back to Ulford, where we found our captain and the crew, who had been picked up by a ship after they 'd been three or four days in their boats. This ship had sailed our way to find us, which, of course, she couldn't do, as at that time we were under water and out of sight.

"And now, sir," said the brother-in-law of J. George Watts to the Shipwreck Clerk, "to which of your classes does this wreck of mine belong?"

"Gents," said the Shipwreck Clerk, rising from his seat, "it 's four o'clock, and at that hour this office closes."

MR. TOLMAN.

MR. TOLMAN.

MR. TOLMAN was a gentleman whose apparent age was of a varying character. At times, when deep in thought on business matters or other affairs, one might have thought him fifty-five or fifty-seven, or even sixty. Ordinarily, however, when things were running along in a satisfactory and commonplace way, he appeared to be about fifty years old, while upon some extraordinary occasions, when the world assumed an unusually attractive aspect, his age seemed to run down to forty-five or less.

He was the head of a business firm; in fact he was the only member of it. The firm was known as Pusey and Co.; but Pusey had long been dead, and the "Co.," of which Mr. Tolman had been a member, was dissolved. Our elderly hero having bought out the business, firm name and all, for many years had carried it on with success and profit. His counting-house was a small and quiet place, but a great deal of

money had been made in it. Mr. Tolman
was rich—very rich indeed.

And yet as he sat in his counting-room
one winter evening he looked his oldest. He
had on his hat and his overcoat, his gloves
and his fur collar. Every one else in the
establishment had gone home ; and he, with
the keys in his hand, was ready to lock up
and leave also. He often stayed later than
any one else, and left the keys with Mr.
Canterfield, the head clerk, as he passed his
house on his way home.

Mr. Tolman seemed in no hurry to go. He
simply sat and thought, and increased his
apparent age. The truth was he did not
want to go home. He was tired of going
home. This was not because his home was
not a pleasant one. No single gentleman in
the city had a handsomer or more comfortable suite of rooms. It was not because he
felt lonely, or regretted that a wife and
children did not brighten and enliven his
home. He was perfectly satisfied to be a
bachelor. The conditions suited him exactly.
But, in spite of all this, he was tired of
going home.

"I wish," said Mr. Tolman to himself,
"that I could feel some interest in going
home ;"and then he rose and took a turn or two

up and down the room ; but as that did not seem to give him any more interest in the matter, he sat down again. "I wish it were necessary for me to go home," said he ; "but it isn't ;" and then he fell again to thinking. "What I need," he said, after a while, "is to depend more upon myself—to feel that I am necessary to myself. Just now I 'm not. I 'll stop going home—at least in this way. Where 's the sense in envying other men, when I can have all that they have, just as well as not ? And I 'll have it, too," said Mr. Tolman, as he went out and locked the doors. Once in the streets, and walking rapidly, his ideas shaped themselves easily and readily into a plan which, by the time he reached the house of his head clerk, was quite matured. Mr. Canterfield was just going down to dinner as his employer rang the bell, so he opened the door himself. "I will detain you but a minute or two," said Mr. Tolman, handing the keys to Mr. Canterfield. "Shall we step into the parlour ?'

When his employer had gone, and Mr. Canterfield had joined his family at the dinner-table, his wife immediately asked him what Mr. Tolman wanted.

"Only to say that he is going away to-morrow, and that I am to attend to the business, and send his personal letters to ——," naming a city not a hundred miles away.

" How long is he going to stay ? "

" He didn't say," answered Mr. Canterfield.

" I 'll tell you what he ought to do," said the lady. " He ought to make you a partner in the firm, and then he could go away and stay as long as he pleased."

" He can do that now," returned her husband. " He has made a good many trips since I have been with him, and things have gone on very much in the same way as when he was here. He knows that."

" But still you 'd like to be a partner ? "

" Oh yes," said Mr. Canterfield.

" And common gratitude ought to prompt him to make you one," said his wife.

Mr. Tolman went home and wrote a will. He left all his property, with the exception of a few legacies, to the richest and most powerful charitable organisation in the country.

" People will think I 'm crazy," said he to himself ; " and if I should die while I am carrying out my plan, I 'll leave the task of defending my sanity to people who are able

to make a good fight for me." And before
he went to bed he had his will signed and
witnessed.

The next day he packed a trunk and left
for the neighbouring city. His apartments
were to be kept in readiness for his return
at any time. If you had seen him walking
over to the railroad dépôt, you would have
taken him for a man of forty-five.

When he arrived at his destination, Mr.
Tolman established himself temporarily at a
hotel, and spent the next three or four days
in walking about the city looking for what
he wanted. What he wanted was rather
difficult to define, but the way in which he
put the matter to himself was something
like this—

"I 'd like to find a snug little place where
I can live and carry on some business which
I can attend to myself, and which will bring
me into contact with people of all sorts—
people who will interest me. It must be a
small business, because I don't want to have to
work very hard, and it must be snug and comfortable, because I want to enjoy it. I would
like a shop of some sort, because that brings
a man face to face with his fellow-creatures."

The city in which he was walking about
was one of the best places in the country in

which to find the place of business he desired. It was full of independent little shops. But Mr. Tolman could not readily find one which resembled his ideal. A small dry-goods establishment seemed to presuppose a female proprietor. A grocery store would give him many interesting customers; but he did not know much about groceries, and the business did not appear to him to possess any æsthetic features. He was much pleased by a small shop belonging to a taxidermist. It was exceedingly cosy, and the business was probably not so great as to overwork any one. He might send the birds and beasts which were brought to be stuffed to some practical operator, and have him put them in proper condition for the customers. He might—— But no; it would be very unsatisfactory to engage in a business of which he knew absolutely nothing. A taxidermist ought not to blush with ignorance when asked some simple question about a little dead bird or a defunct fish. And so he tore himself from the window of this fascinating place, where, he fancied, had his education been differently managed, he could in time have shown the world the spectacle of a cheerful and unblighted Mr. Venus.

The shop which at last appeared to suit him best was one which he had passed and looked at several times before it struck him favourably. It was in a small brick house in a side street, but not far from one of the main business avenues of the city. The shop seemed devoted to articles of stationery and small notions of various kinds not easy to be classified. He had stopped to look at three penknives fastened to a card, which was propped up in the little show-window, supported on one side by a chess-board with "History of Asia" in gilt letters on the back, and on the other by a small violin labelled "1 dollar;" and as he gazed past these articles into the interior of the shop, which was now lighted up, it gradually dawned upon him that it was something like his ideal of an attractive and interesting business place. At any rate he would go in and look at it. He did not care for a violin, even at the low price marked on the one in the window, but a new pocket-knife might be useful; so he walked in and asked to look at pocket-knives.

The shop was in charge of a very pleasant old lady of about sixty, who sat sewing behind the little counter. While she went to the window, and very carefully reached over the articles displayed therein to get the card of penknives, Mr. Tolman looked about him. The shop was quite small, but there seemed to be a good deal in it. There were shelves behind the counter, and there were shelves on the opposite wall, and they all seemed well filled with something or other. In the corner near the old lady's chair was a little coal stove with a bright fire in it, and at the back of the shop, at the top of two steps, was a glass door partly open, through which he saw a small room, with a red carpet on the floor, and a little table apparently set for a meal.

Mr. Tolman looked at the knives when the old lady showed them to him, and after a good deal of consideration he selected one which he thought would be a good knife to give to a boy. Then he looked over some things in the way of paper-cutters, whist-markers, and such small matters, which were in a glass case on the counter; and while he looked at them he talked to the old lady.

She was a friendly, sociable body, and very glad to have any one to talk to, and so it was not at all difficult for Mr. Tolman, by some general remarks, to draw from her a great many points about herself and her shop. She was a widow, with a son who, from her remarks, must have been forty years old. . He was connected with a mercantile establishment, and they had lived here for a long time. While her son was a salesman, and came home every evening, this was very pleasant; but after he became a commercial traveller, and was away from the city for months at a time, she did not like it at all. It was very lonely for her.

Mr. Tolman's heart rose within him, but he did not interrupt her.

"If I could do it," said she, "I would give up this place, and go and live with my sister in the country. It would be better for both of us, and Henry could come there just as well as here when he gets back from his trips."

"Why don't you sell out?" asked Mr. Tolman, a little fearfully, for he began to think that all this was too easy sailing to be entirely safe.

"That would not be easy," said she, with a smile. "It might be a long time before we could find any one who would want to take the place. We have a fair trade in the store, but it isn't what it used to be when times were better; and the library is falling off too. Most of the books are getting pretty old, and it don't pay to spend much money for new ones now."

"The library!" said Mr. Tolman. "Have you a library?"

"Oh yes," replied the old lady. "I've had a circulating library here for nearly fifteen years. There it is, on those two upper shelves behind you."

Mr. Tolman turned, and beheld two long rows of books, in brown paper covers, with a short step-ladder standing near the door of the inner room, by which these shelves might be reached. This pleased him greatly. He had had no idea that there was a library here.

"I declare!" said he. "It must be very pleasant to manage a circulating library—a small one like this, I mean. I shouldn't mind going into a business of the kind myself."

The old lady looked up, surprised. Did he wish to go into business? She had not supposed that, just from looking at him.

Mr. Tolman explained his views to her. He did not tell what he had been doing in the way of business, or what Mr. Canterfield was doing for him now. He merely stated his present wishes, and acknowledged to her that it was the attractiveness of her establish-ment that had led him to come in.

"Then you do not want the penknife?"
she said quickly.

"Oh yes, I do," said he; "and I really
believe, if we can come to terms, that I
would like the two other knives, together
with the rest of your stock in trade."

The old lady laughed a little nervously.
She hoped very much indeed that they
could come to terms. She brought a chair
from the back room, and Mr. Tolman sat
down with her by the stove to talk it over.
Few customers came in to interrupt them,
and they talked the matter over very
thoroughly. They both came to the conclusion that there would be no difficulty
about terms, nor about Mr. Tolman's ability
to carry on the business after a very little
instruction from the present proprietress.
When Mr. Tolman left, it was with the
understanding that he was to call again in
a couple of days, when the son Henry would
be at home, and matters could be definitely
arranged.

When the three met, the bargain was soon
struck. As each party was so desirous of
making it, few difficulties were interposed.
The old lady, indeed, was in favour of some
delay in the transfer of the establishment,
as she would like to clean and dust every

shelf and corner and every article in the place; but Mr. Tolman was in a hurry to take possession; and as the son Henry would have to start off on another trip in a short time, he wanted to see his mother moved and settled before he left. There was not much to move but trunks and bandboxes, and some antiquated pieces of furniture of special value to the old lady, for Mr. Tolman insisted on buying everything in the house, just as it stood. The whole thing did not cost him, he said to himself, as much as some of his acquaintances would pay for a horse. The methodical son Henry took an account of stock, and Mr. Tolman took several lessons from the old lady, in which she explained to him how to find out the selling prices of the various articles from the marks on the little tags attached to them; and she particularly instructed him in the management of the circulating library. She informed him of the character of the books, and, as far as possible, of the character of the regular patrons. She told him whom he might trust to take out a book without paying for the one brought in, if they didn't happen to have the change with them, and she indicated with little crosses opposite their names those persons who should be required to pay cash down for what they had had before receiving further benefits.

It was astonishing to see what interest Mr. Tolman took in all this. He was really anxious to meet some of the people about whom the old lady discoursed. He tried, too, to remember a few of the many things she told him of her methods of buying and selling, and the general management of her shop; and he probably did not forget more than three-fourths of what she told him.

Finally, everything was settled to the satisfaction of the two male parties to the bargain—although the old lady thought of a hundred things she would yet like to do—and one fine frosty afternoon a car-load of furniture and baggage left the door, the old lady and her son took leave of the old place, and Mr. Tolman was left sitting behind the little counter, the sole manager and proprietor of a circulating library and a stationery and notion shop. He laughed when he thought of it, but he rubbed his hands and felt very well satisfied.

"There is nothing really crazy about it," he said to himself. "If there is a thing that I think I would like, and I can afford to have it, and there 's no harm in it, why not have it ?"

There was nobody there to say anything against this ; so Mr. Tolman rubbed his hands again before the fire, and rose to walk up and down his shop, and wonder who would be his first customer.

In the course of twenty minutes a little boy opened the door and came in. Mr. Tolman hastened behind the counter to receive his commands. The little boy wanted two sheets of note-paper and an envelope.

"Any particular kind?" asked Mr. Tolman.

The boy didn't know of any particular variety being desired. He thought the same kind she always got would do ; and he looked very hard at Mr. Tolman, evidently wondering at the change in the shopkeeper, but asking no questions.

"You are a regular customer, I suppose," said Mr. Tolman, opening several boxes of paper which he had taken down from the shelves. "I have just begun business here, and don't know what kind of paper you have been in the habit of buying. But I suppose this will do ;" and he took out a couple of sheets of the best, with an envelope to match. These he carefully tied up in a piece of thin brown paper, and gave to the boy, who handed him three cents. Mr. Tolman took them, smiled, and then having made a rapid calculation, he called to the boy, who was just opening the door, and gave him back one cent.

" You have paid me too much," he said.

The boy took the cent, looked at Mr. Tolman, and then got out of the store as quickly as he could.

" Such profits as that are enormous," said Mr. Tolman ; " but I suppose the small sales balance them." This Mr. Tolman subsequently found to be the case.

One or two other customers came in in the course of the afternoon, and about dark the people who took out books began to arrive. These kept Mr. Tolman very busy. He not only had to do a good deal of entering and cancelling, but he had to answer a great many questions about the change in proprietorship, and the probability of his getting in some new books, with suggestions as to the quantity and character of these, mingled with a few dissatisfied remarks in regard to the volumes already on hand.

Every one seemed sorry that the old lady had gone away ; but Mr. Tolman was so pleasant and anxious to please, and took such an interest in their selection of books, that only one of the subscribers appeared to take the change very much to heart. This was a

young man who was forty-three cents in
arrears. He was a long time selecting a book,
and when at last he brought it to Mr. Tolman
to be entered, he told him in a low voice that
he hoped there would be no objection to let-
ting his account run on for a little while
longer.   On the first of the month he would
settle it, and then he hoped to be able to pay
cash whenever he brought in a book.

Mr. Tolman looked for his name on the
old lady's list, and finding no cross against
it, told him that it was all right, and that
the first of the month would do very well.
The young man went away perfectly satisfied with the new librarian. Thus did Mr.
Tolman begin to build up his popularity.
As the evening grew on he found himself becoming very hungry ; but he did not like to
shut up the shop, for every now and then
some one dropped in, sometimes to ask what
time it was, and sometimes to make a little
purchase, while there were still some library
patrons coming in at intervals.

However, taking courage during a short
rest from customers, he put up the shutters,
locked the door, and hurried off to a hotel,
where he partook of a meal such as few
keepers of little shops ever think of indulg-
ing in.

The next morning Mr. Tolman got his own breakfast. This was delightful. He had seen how cosily the old lady had spread her table in the little back room, where there was a stove suitable for any cooking he might wish to indulge in, and he longed for such a cosy meal. There were plenty of stock provisions in the house, which he had purchased with the rest of the goods ; and he went out and bought himself a fresh loaf of bread. . Then he broiled a piece of ham, made some good strong tea, boiled some eggs, and had a breakfast on the little round table, which, though plain enough, he enjoyed more than any breakfast at his club which he could remember. He had opened the shop, and sat facing the glass door, hoping, almost, that there would be some interruption to his meal. It would seem so much more proper in that sort of business if he had to get up and go and attend to a customer.

Before evening of that day Mr. Tolman became convinced that he would soon be obliged to employ a boy or some one to attend to the establishment during his absence. After breakfast, a woman recommended by the old lady came to make his bed and clean up generally, but when she had gone he was left alone with his shop. He determined not to allow this responsibility to injure his health, and so at one o'clock boldly locked the shop door and went out to his lunch.

He hoped that no one would call during his absence, but when he returned he found a little girl with a pitcher standing at the door. She came to borrow half a pint of milk.

"Milk !" exclaimed Mr. Tolman, in surprise. "Why, my child, I have no milk. I don't even use it in my tea."

The little girl looked very much disappointed. "Is Mrs. Walker gone away for good ?" said she.

"Yes," replied Mr. Tolman. "But I would be just as willing to lend you the milk as she would be, if I had any. Is there any place near here where you can buy milk ? "

"Oh yes," said the girl; "you can get it round in the market-house."

"How much would half a pint cost ?" he asked.

"Three cents," replied the girl.

"Well, then," said Mr. Tolman, "here are three cents. You can go and buy the milk for me, and then you can borrow it. Will that suit ? "

The girl thought it would suit very well, and away she went.

Even this little incident pleased Mr. Tolman. It was so very novel. When he came
back from his dinner in the evening, he
found two circulating library subscribers
stamping their feet on the door-step, and
he afterward heard that several others had
called and gone away. It would certainly
injure the library if he suspended business
at meal-times. He could easily have his
choice of a hundred boys if he chose to
advertise for one, but he shrank from having
a youngster in the place. It would interfere
greatly with his cosiness and his experiences.
He might possibly find a boy who went to
school, and who would be willing to come at
noon and in the evening if he were paid
enough. But it would have to be a very
steady and responsible boy. He would think
it over before taking any steps.

He thought it over for a day or two, but he
did not spend his whole time in doing so.
When he had no customers, he sauntered
about in the little parlour over the shop, with
its odd old furniture, its quaint prints on the
walls, and its absurd ornaments on the mantel-piece. The other little rooms seemed
almost as funny to him, and he was sorry
when the bell on the shop door called him
down from their contemplation. It was

pleasant to him to think that he owned all these odd things. The ownership of the varied goods in the shop also gave him an agreeable feeling, which none of his other possessions had ever afforded him. It was all so odd and novel.

He liked much to look over the books in the library. Many of them were old novels, the names of which were familiar enough to him, but which he had never read. He determined to read some of them as soon as he felt fixed and settled.

In looking over the book in which the names and accounts of the subscribers were entered, he amused himself by wondering what sort of persons they were who had out certain books. Who, for instance, wanted to read *The Book of Cats*; and who could possibly care for *The Mysteries of Udolpho?* But the unknown person in regard to whom Mr. Tolman felt the greatest curiosity was the subscriber who now had in his possession a volume entitled *Dormstock's Logarithms of the Diapason*.

"How on earth," exclaimed Mr. Tolman, "did such a book get into this library; and where on earth did the person spring from who would want to take it out? And not only want to take it," he continued, as he examined the entry regarding the volume, "but come and have it renewed one, two, three, four—nine times ! He has had that book for eighteen weeks !"

Without exactly making up his mind to do so, Mr. Tolman deferred taking steps toward getting an assistant until P. Glascow, the person in question, should make an appearance, and it was nearly time for the book to be brought in again.

"If I get a boy now," thought Mr. Tolman, "Glascow will be sure to come and bring the book while I am out."

In almost exactly two weeks from the date of the last renewal of the book, P. Glascow came in. It was the middle of the afternoon, and Mr. Tolman was alone. This investigator of musical philosophy was a quiet young man of about thirty, wearing a light brown cloak, and carrying under one arm a large book.

P. Glascow was surprised when he heard of the change in the proprietorship of the library. Still he hoped that there would be no objection to his renewing the book which he had with him, and which he had taken out some time ago.

"Oh no," said Mr. Tolman, " none in the world. In fact, I don't suppose there are any other subscribers who would want it. I have had the curiosity to look to see if it had ever been taken out before, and I find it has not."

The young man smiled quietly. "No," said he, "I suppose not. It is not every one who would care to study the higher mathematics of music, especially when treated as Dormstock treats the subject."

"He seems to go into it pretty deeply," remarked Mr. Tolman, who had taken up the book. "At least I should think so, judging from all these calculations, and problems, and squares, and cubes."

"Indeed he does," said Glascow; "and although I have had the book some months, and have more reading-time at my disposal than most persons, I have only reached the fifty-sixth page, and doubt if I shall not have to review some of that before I can feel that I thoroughly understand it."

"And there are three hundred and forty pages in all," said Mr. Tolman compassionately.

"Yes," replied the other; "but I am quite sure that the matter will grow easier as I proceed. I have found that out from what I have already done."

"You say you have a good deal of leisure?"

remarked Mr. Tolman. "Is the musical business dull at present?"

"Oh, I 'm not in the musical business," said Glascow. "I have a great love for music, and wish to thoroughly understand it; but my business is quite different. I am a night druggist, and that is the reason I have so much leisure for reading."

"A night druggist?" repeated Mr. Tolman inquiringly.

"Yes, sir," said the other. "I am in a large down town drug-store, which is kept open all night, and I go on duty after the day-clerks leave."

"And does that give you more leisure?" asked Mr. Tolman.

"It seems to," answered Glascow. "I sleep until about noon, and then I have the rest of the day, until seven o'clock, to myself. I think that people who work at night can make a more satisfactory use of their own time than those who work in the day-time. In the summer I can take a trip on the river, or go somewhere out of town, every day, if I like."

"Daylight is more available for many things, that is true," said Mr. Tolman. "But is it not dreadfully lonely sitting in a drug-store all night? There can't be many people to come to buy medicine at night.　I thought there was generally a night-bell to drug-stores, by which a clerk could be awakened if anybody wanted anything."

"It's not very lonely in our store at night," said Glascow.　"In fact it's often more lively then than in the daytime.　You see, we are right down among the newspaper offices, and there's always somebody coming in for soda-water, or cigars, or something or other.　The store is a bright, warm place for the night editors and reporters to meet together and talk and drink hot soda, and there's always a knot of 'em around the stove about the time the papers begin to go to press.　And they're a lively set, I can tell you, sir.　I've heard some of the best stories I ever heard in my life told in our place after three o'clock in the morning."

"A strange life!" said Mr. Tolman.　"Do you know, I never thought that people amused themselves in that way.　And night after night, I suppose."

"Yes, sir, night after night, Sundays and all."

The night druggist now took up his book.

"Going home to read?" asked Mr. Tolman.

"Well, no," said the other; "it's rather

cold this afternoon to read. I think I 'll
take a brisk walk."

"Can't you leave your book until you
return?" asked Mr. Tolman; "that is, if
you will come back this way. It 's an awkward book to carry about."

"Thank you, I will," said Glascow. "I
shall come back this way."

When he had gone, Mr. Tolman took up
the book, and began to look over it more
carefully than he had done before. But his
examination did not last long.

" How anybody of common sense can take
any interest in this stuff is beyond my com-
prehension," said Mr. Tolman, as he closed
the book and put it on a little shelf behind
the counter.

When Glascow came back, Mr. Tolman
asked him to stay and warm himself; and
then, after they had talked for a short time,
Mr. Tolman began to feel hungry. He had
his winter appetite, and had lunched early.
So said he to the night druggist, who had
opened his " Dormstock," " How would you
like to sit here and read a while, while I go
and get my dinner? I will light the gas,
and you can be very comfortable here, if you
are not in a hurry."

P. Glascow was in no hurry at all, and

was very glad to have some quiet reading by a warm fire; and so Mr. Tolman left him, feeling perfectly confident that a man who had been allowed by the old lady to renew a book nine times must be perfectly trustworthy.

When Mr. Tolman returned, the two had some further conversation in the corner by the little stove.

"It must be rather annoying," said the night druggist, "not to be able to go out to your meals without shutting up your shop. If you like," said he, rather hesitatingly, "I will step in about this time in the afternoon, and stay here while you go to dinner. I'll be glad to do this until you get an assistant. I can easily attend to most people who come in, and others can wait."

Mr. Tolman jumped at this proposition. It was exactly what he wanted.

So P. Glascow came every afternoon and read "Dormstock" while Mr. Tolman went to dinner; and before long he came at lunch-time also. It was just as convenient as not, he said. He had finished his breakfast, and would like to read a while. Mr. Tolman fancied that the night druggist's lodgings were, perhaps, not very well warmed, which idea explained the desire to walk rather than read on a cold afternoon. Glascow's name was entered on the free list, and he always took away the "Dormstock" at night, because he might have a chance of looking into it at the store, when custom began to grow slack in the latter part of the early morning.

One afternoon there came into the shop a young lady, who brought back two books which she had had for more than a month. She made no excuses for keeping the books longer than the prescribed time, but simply handed them in and paid her fine. Mr. Tolman did not like to take this money, for it was the first of the kind he had received ; but the young lady looked as if she was well able to afford the luxury of keeping books over their time, and business was business. So he gravely gave her her change. Then she said she would like to take out *Dormstock's Logarithms of the Diapason.*

Mr. Tolman stared at her. She was a bright, handsome young lady, and looked as if she had very good sense. He could not understand it. But he told her the book was out.

"Out !" she said. "Why, it's always out. It seems strange to me that there

L. or T
o

should be such a demand for that book. I have been trying to get it for ever so long."

"It *is* strange," said Mr. Tolman; "but it is certainly in demand. Did Mrs. Walker ever make you any promises about it?"

"No," said she; "but I thought my turn would come around some time. And I particularly want the book just now."

Mr. Tolman felt somewhat troubled. He knew that the night druggist ought not to monopolise the volume, and yet he did not wish to disoblige one who was so useful to him, and who took such an earnest interest in the book. And he could not temporise with the young lady, and say that he thought the book would soon be in. He knew it would not. There were three hundred and forty pages of it. So he merely remarked that he was sorry.

"So am I," said the young lady, "very sorry. It so happens that just now I have a peculiar opportunity for studying that book, which may not occur again."

There was something in Mr. Tolman's sympathetic face which seemed to invite her confidence, and she continued.

"I am a teacher," she said, "and on account of certain circumstances I have a holiday for a month, which I intended to give up almost entirely to the study of music, and I particularly wanted 'Dormstock.' Do you think there is any chance of its early return, and will you reserve it for me?"

"Reserve it!" said Mr. Tolman. "Most certainly I will." And then he reflected a second or two. "If you will come here the day after to-morrow, I will be able to tell you something definite."

She said she would come.

Mr. Tolman was out a long time at lunch-time the next day. He went to all the leading book-stores to see if he could buy a copy of Dormstock's great work. But he was unsuccessful. The booksellers told him that there was no probability that he could get a copy in the country, unless, indeed, he found it in the stock of some second-hand dealer. There was no demand at all for it, and that if he even sent for it to England, where it was published, it was not likely he could get it, for it had been long out of print. The next day he went to several second-hand stores, but no "Dormstock" could he find.

When he came back he spoke to Glascow on the subject. He was sorry to do so, but thought that simple justice compelled him to mention the matter. The night druggist was thrown into a perturbed state of mind by the information that some one wanted his beloved book.

"A woman!" he exclaimed.   "Why, she would not understand two pages out of the whole of it. It is too bad. I didn't suppose any one would want this book."

"Do not disturb yourself too much," said Mr. Tolman.   "I am not sure that you ought to give it up."

"I am very glad to hear you say so," said Glascow.   "I have no doubt it is only a passing fancy with her. I dare say she would really rather have a good new novel;" and then, having heard that the lady was expected that afternoon, he went out to walk, with the "Dormstock" under his arm.

When the young lady arrived, an hour or so later, she was not at all satisfied to take out a new novel, and was very sorry indeed not to find the *Logarithms of the Diapason* waiting for her. Mr. Tolman told her that he had tried to buy another copy of the work, and for this she expressed herself gratefully. He also found himself compelled to say that the book was in the possession of a gentleman who had had it for some time—all the time it had been out, in fact— and had not yet finished it.

At this the young lady seemed somewhat nettled.

"Is it not against the rules for any person to keep one book out so long?" she asked.

"No," said Mr. Tolman. "I have looked into that. Our rules are very simple, and merely say that a book may be renewed by the payment of a certain sum."

"Then I am never to have it?" remarked the young lady.

"Oh, I wouldn't despair about it," said Mr. Tolman. "He has not had time to reflect upon the matter. He is a reasonable young man, and I believe that he will be willing to give up his study of the book for a time, and let you take it."

"No," said she, "I don't wish that. If he is studying, as you say he is, day and night, I do not wish to interrupt him. I should want the book at least a month, and that, I suppose, would upset his course of study entirely. But I do not think any one should begin in a circulating library to study a book that will take him a year to finish; for, from what you say, it will take this gentleman at least that time to finish Dormstock's book." And so she went her way.

When P. Glascow heard all this in the

evening, he was very grave. He had evidently been reflecting.

"It is not fair," said he. "I ought not to keep the book so long. I now give it up for a while. You may let her have it when she comes." And he put the "Dormstock" on the counter, and went and sat down by the stove.

Mr. Tolman was grieved. He knew the night druggist had done right, but still he was sorry for him. "What will you do?" he asked. "Will you stop your studies?"

"Oh no," said Glascow, gazing solemnly into the stove. "I will take up some other books on the diapason which I have, and will so keep my ideas fresh on the subject until this lady is done with the book. I do not really believe she will study it very long." And then he added: "If it is all the same to you, I will come around here and read, as I have been doing, until you shall get a regular assistant."

Mr. Tolman would be delighted to have him come, he said. He had entirely given up the idea of getting an assistant; but this he did not say.

It was some time before the lady came back, and Mr. Tolman was afraid she was not coming at all. But she did come, and asked for Mrs. Burney's *Evelina.* She smiled when she named the book, and said that she believed she would have to take a novel after all, and she had always wanted to read that one.

"I wouldn't take a novel if I were you," said Mr. Tolman; and he triumphantly took down the "Dormstock" and laid it before her.

She was evidently much pleased, but when he told her of Mr. Glascow's gentlemanly conduct in the matter, her countenance instantly changed.

"Not at all," said she, laying down the book; "I will not break up his study. I will take the *Evelina*, if you please."

And as no persuasion from Mr. Tolman had any effect upon her, she went away with Mrs. Burney's novel in her muff.

"Now, then," said Mr. Tolman to Glascow, in the evening, "you may as well take the book along with you. She won't have it."

But Glascow would do nothing of the kind. "No," he remarked, as he sat looking into the stove; "when I said I would let her have it, I meant it. She'll take it when she sees that it continues to remain in the library."

Glasgow was mistaken: she did not take it, having the idea that he would soon conclude that it would be wiser for him to read it than to let it stand idly on the shelf.

"It would serve them both right," said Mr. Tolman to himself, "if somebody else would come and take it." But there was no one else among his subscribers who would even think of such a thing.

One day, however, the young lady came in and asked to look at the book. "Don't think that I am going to take it out," she said, noticing Mr. Tolman's look of pleasure as he handed her the volume. "I only wish to see what he says on a certain subject which I am studying now;" and so she sat down by the stove, on the chair which Mr. Tolman placed for her, and opened "Dorm-stock."

She sat earnestly poring over the book for half an hour or more, and then she looked up and said, "I really cannot make out what this part means. Excuse my troubling you, but I would be very glad if you would explain the latter part of this passage."

"Me!" exclaimed Mr. Tolman; "why, my good madam—miss, I mean—I couldn't explain it to you if it were to save my life.

But what page is it?" said he, looking at his watch.

"Page twenty-four," answered the young lady.

"Oh, well, then," said he, "if you can wait ten or fifteen minutes, the gentleman who has had the book will be here, and I think he can explain anything in the first part of the work."

The young lady seemed to hesitate whether to wait or not; but as she had a certain curiosity to see what sort of a person he was who had been so absorbed in the book, she concluded to sit a little longer and look into some other parts of the book.

The night druggist soon came in; and when Mr. Tolman introduced him to the lady, he readily agreed to explain the passage to her if he could. So Mr. Tolman got him a chair from the inner room, and he also sat down by the stove.

The explanation was difficult, but it was achieved at last; and then the young lady broached the subject of leaving the book unused. This was discussed for some time, but came to nothing, although Mr. Tolman put down his afternoon paper and joined in the argument, urging, among other points, that as the matter now stood he was deprived by the dead-lock of all income from the book. But even this strong argument proved of no avail.

"Then I'll tell you what I wish you would do," said Mr. Tolman, as the young lady rose to go; "come here and look at the book whenever you wish to do so. I'd like to make this more of a reading-room anyway. It would give me more company."

After this the young lady looked into "Dormstock" when she came in; and as her holidays had been extended by the continued absence of the family in which she taught, she had plenty of time for study, and came quite frequently. She often met with Glascow in the shop; and on such occasions they generally consulted "Dormstock," and sometimes had quite lengthy talks on musical matters. One afternoon they came in together, having met on their way to the library, and entered into a conversation on diapasonic logarithms, which continued during the lady's stay in the shop.

"The proper thing," thought Mr. Tolman, "would be for these two people to get married. Then they could take the book and study it to their hearts' content. And they would certainly suit each other, for they are both greatly attached to musical mathematics and philosophy, and neither of them either plays or sings, as they have told me. It would be an admirable match."

Mr. Tolman thought over this matter a good deal, and at last determined to mention it to Glascow. When he did so, the young man coloured, and expressed the opinion that it would be of no use to think of such a thing. But it was evident from his manner and subsequent discourse that he had thought of it.

Mr. Tolman gradually became quite anxious on the subject, especially as the night druggist did not seem inclined to take any steps in the matter. The weather was now beginning to be warmer, and Mr. Tolman reflected that the little house and the little shop were probably much more cosy and comfortable in winter than in summer. There were higher buildings all about the house, and even now he began to feel that the circulation of air would be quite as agreeable as the circulation of books. He thought a good deal about his airy rooms in the neighbouring city.

"Mr. Glascow," said he, one afternoon, "I have made up my mind to shortly sell out this business."

"What!" exclaimed the other. "Do

you mean you will give it up and go away—
leave the place altogether?"

"Yes," replied Mr. Tolman, "I shall give
up the place entirely, and leave the city."

The night druggist was shocked. He had
spent many happy hours in that shop, and
his hours there were now becoming pleasanter than ever. If Mr. Tolman went
away, all this must end. Nothing of the
kind could be expected of any new proprietor.

"And considering this," continued Mr.
Tolman, "I think it would be well for you
to bring your love matters to a conclusion
while I am here to help you."

"My love matters!" exclaimed Mr. Glascow, with a flush.

"Yes, certainly," said Mr. Tolman. "I
have eyes, and I know all about it. Now
let me tell you what I think. When a thing
is to be done, it ought to be done the first
time there is a good chance. That's the way
I do business. Now you might as well come
around here to-morrow afternoon, prepared
to propose to Miss Edwards. She is due to-
morrow, for she has been two days away.
If she don't come, we'll postpone the matter
until the next day. But you should be
ready to-morrow. I don't believe you can

see her much when you don't meet her here;
for that family is expected back very soon,
and from what I infer from her account of
her employers, you won't care to visit her at
their house."

The night druggist wanted to think about
it.

"There is nothing to think," said Mr.
Tolman. "We know all about the lady."
(He spoke truly, for he had informed himself
about both parties to the affair.) "Take
my advice, and be here to-morrow afternoon
—and come rather early."

The next morning Mr. Tolman went up to
his parlour on the second floor, and brought
down two blue stuffed chairs, the best he
had, and put them in the little room back of
the shop. He also brought down one or two
knicknacks and put them on the mantel-
piece, and he dusted and brightened up the
room as well as he could. He even covered
the table with a red cloth from the parlour.

When the young lady arrived, he invited
her to walk into the back room to look over
some new books he had just got in. If she
had known he proposed to give up the
business, she would have thought it rather
strange that he should be buying new books.
But she knew nothing of his intentions.

When she was seated at the table whereon the new books were spread, Mr. Tolman stepped outside of the shop door to watch for Glascow's approach. He soon appeared.

"Walk right in," said Mr. Tolman. " She 's in the back room looking over books. I 'll wait here, and keep out customers as far as possible. It 's pleasant, and I want a little fresh air. I 'll give you twenty minutes."

Glascow was pale, but he went in without a word ; and Mr. Tolman, with his hands under his coat-tail, and his feet rather far apart, established a blockade on the door-step. He stood there for some time looking at the people outside, and wondering what the people inside were doing. The little girl who had borrowed the milk of him, and who had never returned it, was about to pass the door ; but seeing him standing there, she crossed over to the other side of the street. But he did not notice her. He was wondering if it was time to go in. A boy came up to the door, and wanted to know if he kept Easter-eggs. Mr. Tolman was happy to say he did not. When he had allowed the night druggist a very liberal twenty minutes, he went in. As he entered the shop door, giving the bell a very decided ring as he did so, P. Glascow came down the two steps that led from the inner room. His face showed that it was all right with him.

A few days after this, Mr. Tolman sold out his stock, good-will, and fixtures, together with the furniture and lease of the house. And who should he sell out to but to Mr. Glascow! This piece of business was one of the happiest points in the whole affair. There was no reason why the happy couple should not be married very soon, and the young lady was charmed to give up her position as teacher and governess in a family, and come and take charge of that delightful little store and that cunning little house, with almost everything in it that they wanted.

One thing in the establishment Mr. Tolman refused to sell. That was Dormstock's great work. He made the couple a present of the volume, and between two of the earlier pages he placed a bank-note, which in value was very much more than that of the ordinary wedding-gift.

"And what are *you* going to do?" they asked of him, when all these things were settled. And then he told them how he was going back to his business in the neighbouring city, and he told them what it was, and how he had come to manage a circulating library. They did not think him crazy. People who studied the logarithms of the diapason would not be apt to think a man crazy for such a little thing as that.

When Mr. Tolman returned to the establishment of Pusey & Co., he found everything going on very satisfactorily.

"You look ten years younger, sir," said Mr. Canterfield. "You must have had a very pleasant time. I did not think there was enough to interest you in —— for so long a time."

"Interest me!" exclaimed Mr. Tolman. "Why, objects of interest crowded on me. I never had a more enjoyable holiday in my life."

When he went home that evening (and he found himself quite willing to go), he tore up the will he had made. He now felt that there was no necessity for proving his sanity.

PLAIN FISHING.

"WELL, sir," said old Peter, as he came out on the porch with his pipe, "so you come here to go fishin'?"

Peter Gruse was the owner of the farm-house where I had arrived that day, just before supper-time. He was a short, strong-built old man, with a pair of pretty daughters, and little gold rings in his ears. Two things distinguished him from the farmers in the country round about: one was the rings in his ears, and the other was the large and comfortable house in which he kept his pretty daughters. The other farmers in that region had fine large barns for their cattle and horses, but very poor houses for their daughters. Old Peter's earrings were in-directly connected with his house. He had not always lived among those mountains. He had been on the sea, where his ears were decorated, and he had travelled a good deal on land, where he had ornamented his mind with many ideas which were not in general use in the part of his State in which he was born. This house stood a little back from the highroad, and if a traveller wished to be entertained, Peter was generally willing to take him in, provided he had left his wife and family at home. The old man himself had no objection to wives and children, but his two pretty daughters had.

These two young women had waited on their father and myself at supper-time, one continually bringing hot griddle cakes, and the other giving me every opportunity to test the relative merits of the seven different kinds of preserves, which, in little glass plates, covered the unoccupied spaces on the table-cloth. The latter, when she found that there was no further possible way of serving us, presumed to sit down at the corner of the table and begin her supper. But in spite of this apparent humility, which was only a custom of the country, there was that in the general air of the pretty daughters which left no doubt in the mind of the intelligent observer that they stood at the wheel in that house. There was a son of fourteen, who sat at table with us, but he did not appear to count as a member of the family.

" Yes," I answered, " I understood that

there was good fishing hereabouts, and, at any rate, I should like to spend a few days among these hills and mountains."

"Well," said Peter, "there's trout in some of our streams, though not as many as there used to be, and there's hills a plenty, and mountains too, if you choose to walk fur enough. They're a good deal furder off than they look. What did you bring with you to fish with?"

"Nothing at all," I answered. "I was told in the town that you were a great fisherman, and that you could let me have all the tackle I would need."

"Upon my word," said old Peter, resting his pipe-hand on his knee and looking steadfastly at me, "you're the queerest fisherman I've seed yet. Nigh every year, some two or three of 'em stop here in the fishin' season, and there was never a man who didn't bring his jinted pole, and his reels, and his lines, and his hooks, and his drygood flies, and his whisky-flask with a long strap to it. Now, if you want all these things, I haven't got 'em."

"Whatever you use yourself will suit me," I answered.

"All right, then," said he. "I'll do the best I can for you in the mornin'. But it's plain enough to me that you 're not a game fisherman, or you wouldn't come here without your tools."

To this remark I made answer to the effect, that though I was very fond of fishing, my pleasure in it did not depend upon the possession of all the appliances of professional sport.

" Perhaps you think," said the old man, "from the way I spoke, that I don't believe them fellers with the jinted poles can ketch fish, but that ain't so. That old story about the little boy with the pin-hook who ketched all the fish, while the gentleman with the modern improvements, who stood alongside of him, kep' throwin' out his beautiful flies and never got nothin', is a pure lie. The fancy chaps, who must have ev'rythin' jist so, gen'rally gits fish. But for all that, I don't like their way of fishin', and I take no stock in it myself. I 've been fishin', on and off, ever since I was a little boy, and I 've caught nigh every kind there is, from the big jew-fish and cavalyoes down South, to the trout and minnies round about here. But when I ketch a fish, the first thing I do is to try to git him on the hook, and the next thing is to git him out of the water jist as soon as I kin. I don't put in no time worryin' him.   There's only two animals in the world that likes to worry smaller creeturs a good while afore they kill 'em ; one is the cat, and the other is what they call the game fisherman.   This kind of a feller never goes after no fish that don't mind being ketched.   He goes fur them kinds that loves their home in the water and hates most to leave it, and he makes it jist as hard fur 'em as he kin.   What the game fisher likes is the smallest kind of a hook, the thinnest line, and a fish that it takes a good while to weaken.   The longer the weak'nin' business kin be spun out, the more the sport.   The idee is to let the fish think there's a chance fur him to git away.   That's jist like the cat with her mouse.   She lets the little creetur hop off, but the minnit he gits fur enough down, she jabs on him with her claws, and then, if there's any game left in him, she lets him try agen.   Of course the game fisher could have a strong line and a stout pole and git his fish in a good sight quicker, if he wanted to, but that wouldn't be sport.   He couldn't give him the butt and spin him out, and reel him in, and let him jump and run till his pluck is clean worn out.   Now, I likes to git my fish ashore with all the pluck in 'em.   It makes 'em

taste better.   And as fur fun, I 'll be bound
I 've had jist as much of that, and more, too,
than most of these fellers who are so dreadful
anxious to have everythin' jist right, and
think they can't go fishin' till they 've spent
enough money to buy a suit of Sunday
clothes.   As a gen'ral rule they 're a solemn
lot, and work pretty hard at their fun.
When I work I want to be paid fur it, and
when I go in fur fun I want to take it easy
and comfortable.   Now I wouldn't say so
much agen these fellers," said old Peter, as
he arose and put his empty pipe on a little
shelf under the porch-roof, "if it wasn't for
one thing, and that is, that they think that
their kind of fishin' is the only kind worth
considerin'.   The way they look down upon
plain Christian fishin' is enough to rile a
hitchin'-post.   I don't want to say nothin'
agen no man's way of attendin' to his own
affairs, whether it 's kitchen gardenin', or
whether it 's fishin', if he says nothin' agen
my way ; but when he looks down on me,
and grins me, I want to haul myself up, and
grin him, if I kin.   And in this case, I kin.
I s'pose the house-cat and the cat-fisher (by
which I don't mean the man who fishes for
cat-fish) was both made as they is, and they
can't help it ; but that don't give 'em no

right to put on airs before other bein's, who gits their meat with a square kill. Good night. And sence I 've talked so much about it, I 've a mind to go fishin' with you to-morrow myself."

The next morning found old Peter of the same mind, and after breakfast he proceeded to fit me out for a day of what he called "plain Christian trout-fishin'." He gave me a reed rod, about nine feet long, light, strong, and nicely balanced. The tackle he produced was not of the fancy order, but his lines were of fine strong linen, and his hooks were of good shape, clean and sharp, and snooded to the lines with a neatness that indicated the hand of a man who had been where he learned to wear little gold rings in his ears.

"Here are some of these feather insects," he said, "which you kin take along if you like." And he handed me a paper containing a few artificial flies. "They 're pretty nat'ral," he said, "and the hooks is good. A man who come here fishin' gave 'em to me, but I shan't want 'em to-day. At this time of year grasshoppers is the best bait in the kind of place where we 're goin' to fish. The stream, after it comes down from the mountain, runs through half a mile of medder land before it strikes into the woods agen. A grasshopper is a little creetur that's got as much conceit as if his jinted legs was fish-poles, and he thinks he kin jump over this narrer run of water whenever he pleases; but he don't always do it, and them of him that don't git snapped up by the trout that lie along the banks in the medder is floated along into the woods, where there's always fish enough, to come to the second table."

Having got me ready, Peter took his own particular pole, which he assured me he had used for eleven years, and hooking on his left arm a good-sized basket, which his elder pretty daughter had packed with cold meat, bread, butter, and preserves, we started forth for a three-mile walk to the fishing-ground. The day was a favourable one for our purpose, the sky being sometimes over-clouded, which was good for fishing, and also for walking on a highroad; and some-times bright, which was good for effects of mountain scenery. Not far from the spot where old Peter proposed to begin our sport, a small frame-house stood by the roadside, and here the old man halted and entered the open door without knocking or giving so much as a premonitory stamp. I followed, imitating my companion in leaving my pole outside, which appeared to be the only ceremony that the etiquette of those parts required of visitors. In the room we entered, a small man in his shirt sleeves sat mending a basket handle. He nodded to Peter, and Peter nodded to him.

"We've come up a-fishin'," said the old man. "Kin your boys give us some grasshoppers?"

"I don't know that they've got any ready ketched," said he, "for I reckon I used what they had this mornin'. But they kin git you some. Here, Dan, you and Sile go and ketch Mister Gruse and this young man some grasshoppers. Take that mustard-box, and see that you git it full."

Peter and I now took seats, and the conversation began about a black cow which Peter had to sell, and which the other was willing to buy if the old man would trade for sheep, which animals, however, the basket-mender did not appear just at that time to have in his possession. As I was not very much interested in this subject, I walked to the back door and watched two small boys in scanty shirts and trousers, and ragged straw hats, who were darting about in the grass catching grasshoppers, of which insects, judging by the frequent pounces of the boys, there seemed a plentiful supply.

"Got it full?" said their father when the boys came in.

"Crammed," said Dan.

Old Peter took the little can, pressed the top firmly on, put it in his coat-tail pocket, and rose to go. · "You'd better think about that cow, Barney," said he. He said nothing to the boys about the box of bait; but I could not let them catch grasshoppers for us for nothing, and I took a dime from my pocket, and gave it to Dan. Dan grinned, and Sile looked sheepishly happy, and at the sight of the piece of silver an expression of interest came over the face of the father. "Wait a minute," said he, and he went into a little room that seemed to be a kitchen. Returning, he brought with him a small string of trout. "Do you want to buy some fish?" he said. "These is nice fresh ones. I ketched 'em this mornin'."

To offer to sell fish to a man who is just about to go out to catch them for himself might, in most cases, be considered an insult, but it was quite evident that nothing of the kind was intended by Barney. He probably thought that if I bought grasshoppers, I might buy fish. "You kin have 'em for a quarter," he said.

It was derogatory to my pride to buy fish at such a moment, but the man looked very poor, and there was a shade of anxiety on his face which touched me. Old Peter stood by without saying a word. "It might be well," I said, turning to him, "to buy these fish, for we may not catch enough for supper."

"Such things do happen," said the old man.

"Well," said I, "if we have these we will feel safe in any case." And I took the fish and gave the man a quarter. It was not, perhaps, a professional act, but the trout were well worth the money, and I felt that I was doing a deed of charity.

Old Peter and I now took our rods, and crossed the road into an enclosed lot, and thence into a wide stretch of grass land, bounded by hills in front of us and to the right, while a thick forest lay to the left. We had walked but a short distance, when Peter said: "I'll go down into the woods, and try my luck there, and you'd better go along up stream, about a quarter of a mile, to where it's rocky. P'raps you ain't used to fishin' in the woods, and you might git your line cotched. You'll find the trout'll bite in the rough water."

" Where is the stream ?" I asked.

" This is it," he said, pointing to a little brook, which was scarcely too wide for me to step across, "and there's fish right here, but they're hard to ketch, fur they git plenty of good livin', and are mighty sassy about their eatin'. But you kin ketch 'em up there."

Old Peter now went down toward the woods, while I walked up the little stream. I had seen trout-brooks before, but never one so diminutive as this. However, when I came nearer to the point where the stream issued from between two of the foot-hills of the mountains, which lifted their forest-covered heights in the distance, I found it wider and shallower, breaking over its rocky bottom in sparkling little cascades.

Fishing in such a jolly little stream, surrounded by this mountain scenery, and with the privileges of the beautiful situation all to myself, would have been a joy to me if I had had never a bite. But no such ill-luck befell me. Peter had given me the can of grasshoppers after putting half of them into his own bait-box, and these I used with much success. It was grasshopper season,

and the trout were evidently on the look-
out for them. I fished in the ripples under
the little waterfalls ; and every now and
then I drew out a lively trout. Most of
these were of moderate size, and some of
them might have been called small. The
large ones probably fancied the forest shades,
where old Peter went. But all I caught
were fit for the table, and I was very well
satisfied with the result of my sport.

About an hour after noon I began to feel
hungry, and thought it time to look up the
old man, who had the lunch-basket. I
walked down the bank of the brook, and
some time before I reached the woods I
came to a place where it expanded to a
width of about ten feet. The water here
was very clear, and the motion quiet, so that
I could easily see to the bottom, which did
not appear to be more than a foot below the
surface. Gazing into this transparent water,
as I walked, I saw a large trout glide across
the stream, and disappear under the grassy
bank which overhung the opposite side. I
instantly stopped. This was a much larger
fish than any I had caught, and I determined
to try for him.

I stepped back from the bank, so as to be
out of sight, and put a fine grasshopper on

my hook; then I lay, face downward, on the
grass, and worked myself slowly forward
until I could see the middle of the stream;
then quietly raising my pole, I gave my
grasshopper a good swing, as if he had made
a wager to jump over the stream at its
widest part.   But as he certainly would
have failed in such an ambitious endeavour,
especially if he had been caught by a puff
of wind, I let him come down upon the surface of the water, a little beyond the middle
of the brook.   Grasshoppers do not sink
when they fall into the water, and so I kept
this fellow upon the surface, and gently
moved him along, as if, with all the conceit
taken out of him by the result of his ill-
considered leap, he was ignominiously endeavouring to swim to shore.   As I did this,
I saw the trout come out from under the
bank, move slowly toward the grasshopper,
and stop directly under him.   Trembling
with anxiety and eager expectation, I endeavoured to make the movements of the
insect still more natural, and, as far as I
was able, I threw into him a sudden perception of his danger, and a frenzied desire to
get away.   But, either the trout had had all
the grasshoppers he wanted, or he was able,
from long experience, to perceive the differ-

ence between a natural exhibition of emotion and a histrionic imitation of it, for he slowly turned, and, with a few slight movements of his tail, glided back under the bank. In vain did the grasshopper continue his frantic efforts to reach the shore; in vain did he occasionally become exhausted, and sink a short distance below the surface; in vain did he do everything that he knew, to show that he appreciated what a juicy and delicious morsel he was, and how he feared that the trout might yet be tempted to seize him; the fish did not come out again.

Then I withdrew my line, and moved back from the stream. I now determined to try Mr. Trout with a fly, and I took out the paper old Peter Gruse had given me. I did not know exactly what kind of winged insects were in order at this time of the year, but I was sure that yellow butterflies were not particular about just what month it was, so long as the sun shone warmly. I therefore chose that one of Peter's flies which was made of the yellowest feathers, and, removing the snood and hook from my line, I hastily attached this fly, which was provided with a hook quite suitable for my desired prize. Crouching on the grass, I again approached the brook. Gaily flitting above the glassy surface of the water, in all the fancied security of tender youth and innocence, came my yellow fly. Backward and forward over the water he gracefully flew, sometimes rising a little into the air, as if to view the varied scenery of the woods and mountains, and then settling for a moment close to the surface, to better inspect his glittering image as it came up from below, and showing in his every movement his intense enjoyment of summer-time and life.

Out from his dark retreat now came the trout, and settling quietly at the bottom of the brook, he appeared to regard the venture-some insect with a certain interest. But he must have detected the iron barb of vice beneath the mask of blitheful innocence, for, after a short deliberation, the trout turned and disappeared under the bank. As he slowly moved away, he seemed to be bigger than ever. I must catch that fish! Surely he would bite at something. It was quite evident that his mind was not wholly un-susceptible to emotions emanating from an awakening appetite, and I believed that if he saw exactly what he wanted, he would not neglect an opportunity of availing him-self of it. But what did he want? I must certainly find out. Drawing myself back again, I took off the yellow fly, and put on another. This was a white one, with black blotches, like a big miller moth which had fallen into an ink-pot. It was certainly a conspicuous creature, and as I crept forward and sent it swooping over the stream, I could not see how any trout, with a single insectivorous tooth in his head, could fail to rise to such an occasion. But this trout did not rise. He would not even come out from under his bank to look at the swiftly flitting creature. He probably could see it well enough from where he was.

But I was not to be discouraged. I put on another fly ; a green one with a red tail. It did not look like any insect that I had ever seen, but I thought that the trout might know more about such things than I. He did come out to look at it, but probably considering it a product of that modern æstheticism which sacrifices natural beauty to mediæval crudeness of colour and form, he retired without evincing any disposition to countenance this style of art.

It was evident that it would be useless to put on any other flies, for the two I had left were a good deal bedraggled, and not nearly so attractive as those I had used. Just before leaving the house that morning

Peter's son had given me a wooden match-box filled with worms for bait, which, although I did not expect to need, I put in my pocket. As a last resort I determined to try the trout with a worm. I selected the plumpest and most comely of the lot; I put a new hook on my line; I looped him about it in graceful coils, and cautiously approached the water, as before. Now a worm never attempts to wildly leap across a flowing brook, nor does he flit in thoughtless innocence through the sunny air, and over the bright transparent stream. If he happens to fall into the water, he sinks to the bottom; and if he be of a kind not subject to drowning, he generally endeavours to secrete himself under a stone, or to burrow in the soft mud. With this knowledge of his nature I gently dropped my worm upon the surface of the stream, and then allowed him to slowly sink. Out sailed the trout from under the bank, but stopped before reaching the sinking worm. There was a certain something in his action which seemed to indicate a disgust at the sight of such plebeian food, and a fear seized me that he might now swim off, and pay no further attention to my varied baits. Suddenly there was a ripple in the water, and I felt a pull

on the line. Instantly I struck ; and then
there was a tug. My blood boiled through
every vein and artery, and I sprang to my
feet. I did not give him the butt : I did
not let him run with yards of line down the
brook ; nor reel him in, and let him make
another mad course up stream : I did not
turn him over as he jumped into the air ;
nor endeavour, in any way, to show him that
I understood those tricks, which his de-
praved nature prompted him to play upon
the angler. With an absolute dependence
upon the strength of old Peter's tackle, I
lifted the fish. Out he came from the water,
which held him with a gentle suction as if
unwilling to let him go, and then he whirled
through the air like a meteor flecked with
rosy fire, and landed on the fresh green grass
a dozen feet behind me. Down on my knees
I dropped before him as he tossed and rolled,
his beautiful spots and colours glistening in
the sun. He was truly a splendid trout,
fully a foot long, round and heavy. Carefully seizing him, I easily removed the hook
from the bony roof of his capacious mouth
thickly set with sparkling teeth, and then I
tenderly killed him, with all his pluck,
as old Peter would have said, still in him.
I covered the rest of the fish in my basket

with wet plantain leaves, and laid my trout-king on this cool green bed. Then I hurried off to the old man, whom I saw coming out of the woods. When I opened my basket and showed him what I had caught, Peter looked surprised, and, taking up the trout, examined it.

"Why, this is a big fellow," he said. "At first I thought it was Barney Sloat's boss trout, but it isn't long enough for him. Barney showed me his trout, that gen'rally keeps in a deep pool, where a tree has fallen over the stream down there. Barney tells me he often sees him, and he's been tryin' fur two years to ketch him, but he never has, and I say he never will, fur them big trout's got too much sense to fool round any kind of victuals that's got a string to it. They let a little fish eat all he wants, and then they eat him. How did you ketch this one?"

I gave an account of the manner of the capture, to which Peter listened with interest and approval.

"If you'd a stood off and made a cast at that feller, you'd either have caught him at the first flip, which isn't likely, as he didn't seem to want no feather-flies, or else you'd a skeered him away. That's all well enough

in the tumblin' water, where you gen'rally
go fur trout, but the man that 's got the true
feelin' fur fish will try to suit his idees to
theyrn, and if he keeps on doin' that, he 's
like to learn a thing or two that may do
him good. That's a fine fish, and you ketched
him well. I 've got a lot of 'em, but nothin'
of that heft."

After luncheon we fished for an hour or
two, with no result worth recording, and
then we started for home. A couple of
partridges ran across the road some distance ahead of us, and these gave Peter an
idea.

"Do you know," said he, "if things go on
as they 're goin' on now, that there 'll come
a time when it won't be considered high-
toned sport to shoot a bird slam-bang dead.
The game gunners will pop 'em with little
harpoons, with long threads tied to 'em, and
the feller that can tire out his bird, and
haul him in with the longest and thinnest
piece of spool cotton, will be the crackest
sportsman."

At this point I remarked to my companion
that perhaps he was a little hard on the
game fishermen.

"Well," said old Peter, with a smile on
his corrugated visage, "I reckon I 'd have to

do a lot of talkin' before I'd git even with 'em, fur the way they give me the butt for my style of fishin'.　What I say behind their backs I say to their faces.　I seed one of these fellers once with a fish on his hook, that he was runnin' up an' down the stream like a chased chicken.　'Why don't you pull him in?' says I.　'And break my rod an' line?' says he.　'Why don't you have a stronger line and pole?' says I.　'There wouldn't be no science in that,' says he.　'If it's your science you want to show off,' says I, ' you ought to fish for mud eels.　There's more game in 'em than there is in any other fish round here, and as they're mighty lively out of water, you might play one of 'em fur half an hour after you got him on shore, and it would take all your science to keep him from reelin' up his end of the line faster than you could yourn.'"

When we reached the farm the old man went into the barn, and I took the fish into the house.　I found the two pretty daughters in the large room, where the eating and some of the cooking was done.　I opened my basket, and with great pride showed them the big trout I had caught.　They evidently thought it was a large fish, but they looked at each other, and smiled in a way that I did not understand. I had expected from them, at least, as much admiration for my prize and my skill as their father had shown.

"You don't seem to think much of this fine trout that I took such trouble to catch," I remarked.

"You mean," said the elder girl, with a laugh, "that you bought of Barney Sloat."

I looked at her in astonishment.

"Barney was along here to-day," she said, "and he told about your buying your fish of him."

"Bought of him!" I exclaimed indignantly. "A little string of fish at the bottom of the basket I bought of him, but all the others, and this big one, I caught myself."

"Oh, of course," said the pretty daughter, "bought the little ones and caught all the big ones."

"Barney Sloat ought to have kept his mouth shut," said the younger pretty daughter, looking at me with an expression of pity. "He'd got his money, and he hadn't no business to go telling on people. Nobody likes that sort of thing. But this big fish is a real nice one, and you shall have it for your supper."

"Thank you," I said, with dignity, and left the room.

I did not intend to have any further words with these young women on this subject, but I cannot deny that I was annoyed and mortified. This was the result of a charitable action. I think I was never more proud of anything than of catching that trout; and it was a very considerable downfall to suddenly find myself regarded as a mere city man fishing with a silver hook. But, after all, what did it matter? But the more I said this to myself, the more was I impressed with the fact that it mattered a great deal.

The boy who did not seem to be accounted a member of the family came into the house, and as he passed me he smiled good-humouredly, and said: "Buyed 'em!"

I felt like throwing a chair at him, but refrained out of respect to my host. Before supper the old man came out on to the porch where I was sitting. "It seems," said he, "that my gals has got it inter their heads that you bought that big fish of Barney Sloat, and as I can't say I seed you ketch it, they're not willin' to give in, 'specially as I didn't git no such big one. 'Tain't wise to buy fish when you're goin' fishin' yourself. It's pretty certain to tell agen you."

"You ought to have given me that advice before," I said, somewhat shortly. "You saw me buy the fish."

"You don't s'pose," said old Peter, "that I'm goin' to say anythin' to keep money out of my neighbour's pockets. We don't do that way in these parts. But I've told the gals they're not to speak another word about it, so you needn't give your mind no worry on that score. And now let's go in to supper. If you're as hungry as I am, there won't be many of them fish left fur breakfast."

That evening, as we were sitting smoking on the porch, old Peter's mind reverted to the subject of the unfounded charge against me. "It goes pretty hard," he remarked, "to have to stand up and take a thing you don't like when there's no call fur it. It's bad enough when there is a call fur it. That matter about your fish buyin' reminds me of what happened two summers ago to my sister, or ruther to her two little boys—or, more correct yit, to one of 'em. Them was two cur'ous little boys. They was allus tradin' with each other. Their father deals mostly in horses, and they must have

got it from him.   At the time I 'm tellin' of
they 'd traded everythin' they had, and when
they hadn't nothin' else left to swap they
traded names.   Joe he took Johnny's name,
and Johnny he took Joe's.   Jist about when
they 'd done this, they both got sick with
sumthin' or other, the oldest one pretty bad,
the other not much. Now there ain't no doctor
inside of twenty miles of where my sister
lives.   But there 's one who sometimes has
a call to go through that part of the country,
and the people about there is allus very glad
when they chance to be sick when he comes
along.   Now this good luck happened to my
sister, fur the doctor come by jist at this
time.   He looks into the state of the boys,
and while their mother has gone downstairs
he mixes some medicine he has along with
him.   ' What 's your name ? ' he says to the
oldest boy when he 'd done it.   Now as he 'd
traded names with his brother, fair and
square, he wasn't goin' back on the trade,
and he said, ' Joe.' ' And my name 's
Johnny,' up and says the other one.   Then
the doctor he goes and gives the bottle of
medicine to their mother, and says he :
' This medicine is fur Joe. You must give
him a tablespoonful every two hours.   Keep
up the treatment, and he 'll be all right.   As

fur Johnny, there 's nothin' much the matter with him. He don't need no medicine.' And then he went away. Every two hours after that Joe, who wasn't sick worth mentionin', had to swaller a dose of horrid stuff, and pretty soon he took to his bed, and Johnny he jist played round and got well in the nat'ral way. Joe's mother kept up the treatment, gittin' up in the night to feed that stuff to him ; but the poor little boy got wuss and wuss, and one mornin' he says to his mother, says he : 'Mother, I guess I'm goin' to die, and I'd ruther do that than take any more of that medicine, and I wish you'd call Johnny and we'll trade names back agen, and if he don't want to come and do it, you kin tell him he kin keep the old minkskin I gave him to boot, on account of his name havin' a Wesley in it.' 'Trade names,' says his mother, 'what do you mean by that?' And then he told her what he and Johnny had done. 'And did you ever tell anybody about this?' says she. 'Nobody but Dr. Barnes,' says he. 'After that I got sick and forgot it.' When my sister heard that, an idee struck into her like you put a fork into an apple dumplin.' Traded names, and told the doctor ! She 'd all along thought it strange that the boy that seemed wuss should be turned out, and the other one put under treatment; but it wasn't fur her to set up her opinion agen that of a man like Dr. Barnes. Down she went, in about seventeen jumps, to where Eli Timmins, the hired man, was ploughin' in the corn. 'Take that horse out of that,' she hollers, 'and you may kill him if you have to, but git Dr. Barnes here before my little boy dies.' When the doctor come he heard the story, and looked at the sick youngster, and then says he: 'If he'd kept his minkskin, and not hankered after a Wesley to his name, he'd a had a better time of it. Stop the treatment, and he'll be all right.' Which she did; and he was. Now it seems to me that this is a good deal like your case. You've had to take a lot of medicine that didn't belong to you, and I guess it's made you feel pretty bad; but I've told my gals to stop the treatment, and you'll be all right in the mornin'. Good night. Your candle-stick is on the kitchen table."

For two days longer I remained in this neighbourhood, wandering alone over the hills, and up the mountain-sides, and by the brooks, which tumbled and gurgled through the lonely forest. Each evening I brought home a goodly supply of trout, but never a great one like the noble fellow for which I angled in the meadow stream.

On the morning of my departure I stood on the porch with old Peter waiting for the arrival of the mail driver, who was to take me to the nearest railroad town.

"I don't want to say nothin'," remarked the old man, "that would keep them fellers with the jinted poles from stoppin' at my house when they comes to these parts a-fishin'. I ain't got no objections to their poles; 'tain't that. And I don't mind nuther their standin' off, and throwin' their flies as fur as they 've a mind to; that 's not it. And it ain't even the way they have of worryin' their fish. I wouldn't do it myself, but if they like it, that 's their business. But what does rile me is the cheeky way in which they stand up and say that there isn't no decent way of fishin' but their way. And that to a man that 's ketched more fish, of more different kinds, with more game in 'em, and had more fun at it, with a lot less money and less tom-foolin' than any fishin' feller that ever come here and talked to me like an old cat tryin' to teach a dog to ketch rabbits. No, sir; agen I say that I don't take no money fur entertainin' the only man that ever come out here to go a-fishin' in a plain, Christian way.

But if you feel tetchy about not payin' nothin', you kin send me one of them poles in three pieces, a good strong one, that 'll lift Barney Sloat's trout, if ever I hook him."

I sent him the rod ; and next summer I am going up to see him use it.

MY BULL-CALF.

L. or T.   R

MY BULL-CALF.

I AM an animal painter, and although I am
not well known to fame, I have painted
a good many pictures, most of which may
now be seen on the walls of my studio. In
justice to myself I must say that the critics
of the Art exhibitions and those persons
competent to judge who have visited my
studio have spoken in praise of my pictures,
and have given me a good place among the
younger artists of the country ; sometimes,
indeed, they have said things about the suggested sentiment of some of my work which
I am too modest here to repeat. But in spite
of this commendation, which I labour hard to
deserve, there has been no great demand for
my paintings.

A facetious brother artist once attempted
to explain the slowness of my sales. "You
see," said he, "that painting changes the
nature of its subjects. In real life animals
frequently go off very rapidly, but when they
are painted they don't."

The same gentleman also made a good deal of fun of one of my first paintings—a dead lion. This animal had died in a menagerie in the city, and having heard of his decease, I bought his remains for five dollars, and after dark I conveyed them to my studio in a wheelbarrow. I was quite young and en-thusiastic then, and as the animal had appa-rently died of a consumption, he was not very heavy. I worked day and night at a life-size (so to speak) portrait of the beast, and it was agreed by all who saw it that I succeeded very well. But no one seemed inclined in the slight-est degree to buy the picture. "What you are waiting for," said my facetious friend, " is the visit of a live ass. When he comes along he will buy that thing, and make your fortune."

My latest work was a life-size picture of a bull-calf. Some time before I determined to devote myself to cattle painting, and had bought a cow for a model. This I did be-cause I found it difficult to have control over the cows of other people. I live a short dis-tance out of town, and while the farmers thereabout were very willing that I should go into the field and sketch their cows, they would not allow me to pen one of them up in a confined space where I could study her form and features without following her, easel and material in hand, over a wide and sometimes marshy pasture. My cow proved a very valuable possession. I rented a small grassy field for her, and put up a cheap and comfortable shed in one corner of it. I sold her milk to the good lady with whom I lived, and my model cow paid all her expenses, attendance included. She was a gentle creature, and becoming accustomed to my presence, would generally remain in one position for a long time, and when I stirred her up would readily assume some other attitude of repose. I did not always copy her exactly. Sometimes I gave her one colour and sometimes another, and sometimes several blended ; at one time I gave her horns, and at another none; and in this way I frequently made a herd of her, scattering her over a verdant mead. I did not always even paint her as a cow. With a different head and branching horns, a longer neck, a thinner body, a shorter tail, and longer legs, she made an excellent stag, the lifelike poses which I was enabled to get giving the real value to the picture. Once I painted her as a sphinx, her body couched in the conventional way, with claws at the ends of the legs instead of hoofs, and a little altered in contour, making an admirable study ; and there was an expression in her eye, as she meditatively crunched a cabbage leaf, which made me give it to the woman's head that I placed upon her.

"What a far-off, prophetic look it has!" said one who stood before the picture when it was finished. "It seems to gaze across the sands of Egypt, and to see things thousands of years ahead. If you could fix up a little bit of sunset in the distance, with some red and yellow clouds in the shape of the flag of England, the symbolised sentiment would be quite perfect."

The bull-calf which afterward served as my model was the son of my cow. When he was old enough to go about by himself and eat hay and grass, I sold his mother at a good profit, and retained him as a model, and the life-size picture of him, on which I worked for a long time, was my masterpiece. When it was nearly finished I brought it to my studio, and there day after day I touched and retouched it, often thinking it finished, but always finding, when I went home and looked at my calf, that there was something of life and truth in the real animal which I had not given to the picture, and which I afterward strove to suggest, if not to copy.

I had a friend who occupied a studio in the same building, and who took a great interest in the portrait of my bull-calf. The specialty of this artist was quiet landscape and flowers, and we had frequently gone into the country and sketched together, the one drawing the cattle, and the other the field in which they roved. One day we stood before my almost completed work.

"What a spirited and lifelike air he has!" remarked my companion. "He looks as if he was just about to hunch up his back, give a couple of awkward skips, and then butt at us. I really feel like shutting the door, when I come in, for fear he should jump down and run away. You are going to brighten up the foreground a little, are you not?"

"Yes," I answered; "and what it needs is a modest cluster of daisies in this corner. Won't you paint them in for me? You can do it so much better than I can!"

"No," she answered; "I positively will not. No one but yourself should touch it. It is your very best work, and it should be all your picture."

In the course of my life I had not had, or at least I believed that I had not had, many of those pieces of good fortune which people call "opportunities." Now here was one, and I determined to seize it. "Why can it not be *our* picture?" I asked.

She looked up at me with a quick glance, which seemed to say, " What ! are you about to speak at last ? "

In ten minutes all had been said, and we were engaged to be married.

Our studios were opposite each other, separated by a wide hall, and it had been our custom, when one went to luncheon, for the other to sit, with open door, so that visitors to the absent one might be seen and attended to. Emma generally lunched at a quiet restaurant near by much frequented by ladies, and where an occasional male visitor might be seen, and to this place I also went as soon as she came back. I knew her favourite little table in the corner, and I always tried to occupy the place she had just vacated. But to-day we determined to lock our studio doors and lunch together. There was really very little reason to expect a visitor. The waiter who attended to our wants was a quiet coloured man, with white hair and whiskers, and an expression of kindly observation on his sable countenance. He arranged our table with much care, and listened to our orders with a deference I had not noticed before ; but perhaps he always waited thus on ladies. While we were eating he retired to a little distance, and stood regarding us with an interested but not too intent attention. We had so often eaten at the same table, but never before at the same time.

When we returned we went first to my studio, and when we opened the door the bull-calf seemed to smile. We both noticed it.

"There is something in the way he looks at us," said Emma, "that reminds me of our old waiter."

"Strange," I replied. "I noticed that myself."

Again I urged her to make the daisies for me, but she still refused.

"No," she said. "It is your picture, and you must not be unable to say that you did it all yourself. And besides, if I were to put in any daisies, your calf is so natural that he would snip them off. I will not have my daisies snipped off, even by that handsome creature."

She looked up, as she said this, with a smile as bright and fresh as any daisy, and I—— But never mind.

The next day we went again together to the restaurant, and the kindly observation deepened on the face of the waiter. When he had arranged with unusual nicety the little table service, he placed before Emma a wine-glass containing a button-hole bouquet. When we were leaving he detained me a moment, and said in a low voice—

"After this, sir, if you would first order your beef for one with two plates, and then order the lady's chicken and salad for one with two plates, you would each have some beef and some chicken. It wouldn't cost any more, sir, and 'twould make more of a *menu.*"

"After this!" I mentally repeated as I gratefully put my hand in my pocket. If that old waiter had been an artist, what a gift his powers of observation would have been to him!

We agreed that we would be married in the early autumn, for truly there was little reason for delay. "It has been so many, many months," I said, "since I declared to myself that I would never marry any one but you, that I really consider that I have been engaged to you for a very long time."

"I may as well admit that something of the same kind has passed through my mind. It is no harm to tell you so now, and it will make more of a *menu.*"

If my calf really cared to snip daisies, he must have envied me then.

There was no impediment to our early

marriage except the fact that neither of us had any money.

"What you must do," said Emma, "is to finish your picture and sell it. You must stop looking at the calf you have at home. Of course he is growing every day, and new beauties are coming out on him all the time. You cannot expect to have his picture keep pace with his development. After a while you will have to give him horns, and make him larger."

"The model is bigger now than the picture," I said; "and I must take your advice, and stop looking at him. If I don't, his portrait will never be done."

I would not put any flowers in the foreground, for, if I did so, I was sure they would look as if they had been picked out of a lady's bonnet. After what I had seen Emma do, I knew I could not paint daisies and buttercups. I put in some pale mullein leaves, and a point of rock which caught the light, and when this was done I determined to call the picture finished.

"What are you going to ask for it?" asked Emma.

"I had thought of a thousand dollars. Don't you consider that is a reasonable price?"

"I think it is a very low price," she answered, "considering the size of the picture
and the admirable way in which it is painted.
I imagine it is seldom that a picture like
that is offered at a thousand dollars ; but, as
you want to sell it very much, I suppose it
will be well not to ask any more."

"I do want very much to sell it," I said,
giving her hand a squeeze which she understood.

I had also made up my mind in regard to
the mode of disposing of the picture. Some
weeks before, an artist friend in Boston had
written to me that a well-known picture-
dealer would open in that city early in
September an art establishment particularly
for the sale of pictures on commission, and
that he would inaugurate his enterprise with
an exhibition of paintings, which he wished to
make as extensive and attractive as possible.

"If you have anything good, finished in
time," wrote my friend, "I think you will
do well to send it to Schemroth. He knows
your work, and, if I mistake not, bought one
of your pictures when he was in business in
New York. I doubt if he has many animal
subjects, and he wants variety. He says he
is going to make his exhibition one of the
art features of the season."

Emma agreed with me that I could not do better than send my picture to Schemroth. He was an enterprising man, and would be certain to do everything he could to attract attention to his exhibition, and she felt sure that if the art public of Boston had a good opportunity of seeing my picture it would certainly be sold.

The painting was carefully packed, and sent to Boston, in care of my friend there, who shortly afterward wrote me that Schemroth liked it, and had given it a good place in his gallery, which would open in a day or two. My studio looked very bare and empty after the departure of my spirited bull-calf, so long my daily companion; but my mind was so occupied with the consideration of the important event which was to follow his sale, that I did not miss him as much as I would otherwise have done. Emma and I talked a good deal about the best way of beginning our married life, and I was much in favour of a trip to Europe; but in regard to this she did not agree with me.

"A thousand dollars," she said, "would not go far for such a purpose. The steamer tickets would cost us about a hundred dollars apiece, and that would be four hundred dollars to go and come back. Then you certainly ought to keep a hundred dollars for your own use before you start, and that would only leave five hundred dollars with which to go to Paris and Rome and Dresden. If we did less than that, it would be hardly worth while to go at all. And five hundred dollars would not begin to be enough for two people."

I was obliged to admit that she was correct, and the European trip was given up.

"My idea is," said Emma, "that we ought to take the money and furnish a house with it. That will be a good practical beginning, and after a while, when we have painted a few more pictures, we can go to Europe. You could keep a hundred dollars for your own use; we could put aside two hundred for rainy days, or whatever kind of weather it may be when money is needed and there is none coming in, and then with seven hundred dollars we could buy enough furniture and other things to begin house-keeping in a small way. By this plan, you see, sir, your beautiful calf would give us an excellent start in life."

This proposition needed no discussion. Before she had half finished speaking I was convinced that nothing could be more sensible and delightful. "We must look for a house immediately," I said. "It won't do to put off that part of the business. We should know where we are going to live, so that when we are ready to buy the furniture there need be no delay."

Good fortunes as well as misfortunes sometimes object to coming singly; and just at this time I heard of something which was certainly a piece of rare good luck to a young couple contemplating matrimony. A gentleman named Osburn, who lived near my country home, with whom I had become well acquainted, and to whom I had confided the important news of my engagement, met me on the train a day or two after Emma and I had agreed upon the furniture project, and told me that if I intended to go to housekeeping he thought he could offer me a desirable opportunity. "My wife and I," he said, "wish very much to travel for a year or two, and the time has now arrived when we can do it, if we can dispose of our household effects, and get some one to take our house, on which we have a lease. Now, if you are going to marry, and care for a place like ours, it might be worth your while to consider the question of taking it and buying our furniture. We will sell everything just as it is, excepting, of course, the books, and

such small articles as have a personal value,
and you can walk right in and begin housekeeping at once.   Everything was new two
years ago, and you know my wife is a very
careful housekeeper. The house is small, and
very simply furnished, and I have no doubt
you would want to add all sorts of things,
but at first you wouldn't really need anything that you wouldn't find there. We wish
to dispose of the whole establishment—linen,
china, silver (it's only plated, but it's very
good), kitchen utensils, garden tools, a lot
of fine poultry, a dog, a cat—everything, in
fact, excepting the few articles I spoke of.
What do you say?"

"Say!" I exclaimed; "there is nothing
to say, except that I should be perfectly delighted to take the place off your hands if I
could afford it; but I am afraid your price
would be above my means. I suppose you
would want to sell all or nothing?"

"Oh yes," said Mr. Osburn; "it would
not pay us to sell out piecemeal, and we do
not wish to let the house to any one who
will not buy the furniture. If you think
the proposition worth considering, my wife
and I will make an estimate of what we
consider the effects worth, and let you
know."

I told him I should be very glad indeed to know, and he said I should hear from him in a day or two.

When I told Emma of this, and described to her the Osburns' house, with its neat and comfortable furniture, its æsthetic wall-paper, its convenient and airy rooms, its well-kept garden and little lawn, its handsome barn and poultry-house, the wide pasture-field belonging to it, the little patch of woodland at the upper end, the neatness and order of everything about the place; and all this at a very moderate rental, with a lease that had several years to run, she agreed with me, that while it would be perfectly delightful to take this ready-made home off the Osburns' hands, there was no reason for us to hope that we should be able to do it. We should have to be content with something far less complete and perfect than this.

Two days after, I received a note from Osburn. "We have carefully considered the present value of our possessions," he said, "with an especial view of making it an object to you to buy them as a whole. Everything is in good order, but as we have had two years' use of the articles, we have considered that fact in making an estimate of what we think we ought to receive for them. After going over the matter several times, we have determined to offer you the furniture and other things of which I spoke to you for seven hundred and fifty dollars."

"Why," cried Emma, as she read this letter over my shoulder (for I had taken it into her studio before I opened it), "that is only fifty dollars more than we had appropriated!"

"But we won't stop for that," I exclaimed.

"Stop!" she said, as with sparkling eyes and glowing cheeks she took both my hands in her own—regardless of the fact that she already held a brush heavily charged with Vandyck brown—"I should think not."

To work any more then was impossible for either of us. That afternoon we shut up both our studios, and went out to look at the paradise which had been offered us. Mr. Osburn had not yet come home, but his wife took great pleasure in making Emma's acquaintance, and in showing us over the house and grounds. We found everything better of its kind, better adapted to the place in which it was, better suited to our every purpose, and altogether ever so much more desirable, than we had thought. I never saw Emma so enthusiastic. Even the picture of my bull-calf had not moved her thus. If the price had not been fixed beforehand, our delighted satisfaction would have been very impolitic. When Mr. Osburn returned I told him without hesitation that I would accept his offer. I think that he and his wife were almost as much pleased as we were. They had set their hearts on an extended tour in the South and far West. The lady's health demanded this, and her husband had found that he could now so arrange his business as to unite travel with profit; but it would have been impossible, as he afterward told me, for him to adopt this new mode of life without first disposing of his furniture and household goods. Ready money, I fancy, was not abundant with him.

When we took leave of the Osburns, four people in very high spirits stood shaking hands in the porch of the pretty house in which we had decided to make our home. There was an extraordinarily good point in this extraordinary piece of good fortune which had befallen us. If the Osburns had wished to settle the business with us at once, it would, of course, have been impossible for us to do our part, but it would be at least six weeks

before they intended to give up their house,
and in that time we felt quite sure that my
picture would be sold.   But although we
could take no actual steps toward making
our arrangements for housekeeping, there
was nothing to prevent our thinking and
talking about them, and planning what was
to be done ; and this occupied a great deal
of our time, much to the detriment, I am
sure, of our daily work.   We were always
finding new good points in the matter.

"The only things about the Osburn house
that I don't like," said Emma, "are the
pictures and the bric-à-brac.   Now these are
the things that they want to keep, and if we
are well off in any way, it is in pictures, and
we can just take some of the paintings we
have on hand, and a lot of our large engrav-
ings, and have them framed, and with that
old armour and brass and china which you
have collected, and which an animal painter
doesn't want in his studio anyway, we can
make our house look just lovely.   I have
collected too, and I have a good many nice
things in my room which you have never
seen."

"The house is a good one now," I exclaimed, "but it will look like another place
when you and I get into it.   And there is

another thing that I have been thinking about. Of course I'll take my calf over there the first thing, and he will get a great deal better eating in that meadow than he has now. But he won't be the only animal we will have. I intend to have a little model farm; that is to say, a farm on which we will keep models. Of course we will have a cow, and she will not only give us milk and butter, but I can paint her. There is a fine little barn and stable on the place, but Osburn says he never thought he ought to keep a horse, because the house is only five minutes from the station, and it would be a piece of sheer extravagance for him to have a horse just to drive about after he came home at night. But it wouldn't be extravagant in me; it would be actual economy. I ought to paint horses, and to do so properly and economically I should own one. And so with all sorts of animals. If I buy a fine dog or a beautiful cat, it will actually be money in my pocket."

"That is true," said Emma; "but you mustn't bring any wild animals there until they are so dead that you can wheel them home in a wheelbarrow. It will be perfectly delightful to have a horse, and as I intend to paint birds as well as flowers, I can begin

on the hens and little chickens and the
ducks; and the sparrows and robins, if I can
make them tame enough for me to sketch
them."

"Yes," I exclaimed, "and you can paint
the wild-flowers in your own field; and
we'll raise splendid Jacqueminot roses, and
the hybrid tea, and other fine kinds; and
we'll fix up a room for them in the winter, so that you can always have flowers
for models at whatever stage you want
them."

In the weeks that followed we paid several
visits to the Osburns by their invitation,
during which the husband explained to me
the management of the celery beds, and
many of his outdoor improvements, while
the wife had some long conversations
with Emma about her household arrangements.

As the time approached when the Osburns
wished to give up their house, Emma and I
became very anxious to hear from Boston.
I had written to my friend there explaining
the situation, and he had promised to attend
to the matter, and see that Schemroth com-
municated with me as soon as the picture
was sold; so there was nothing to do but
wait. I frequently met Mr. Osburn on the

train, and I began to feel, as the time passed on, that I ought to be able to say something to him about concluding our bargain.

Of course he must have his preparations to make, and he would not wish to delay them too long. Although there was no real reason for it, as we assured ourselves over and over, both Emma and I began to be very uneasy, and we sometimes even regretted that we had accepted Mr. Osburn's offer. If we had not complicated the affair in this way, we could have calmly waited until the picture was sold, and have then done what seemed to us best. There was no probability that we would have met with so good an opportunity of going into housekeeping, but we should have been independent, and easy in our minds. But now we were neither. The plans and prospects of others depended upon us, and our uneasiness and anxiety increased every day. I disliked to meet Mr. Osburn, and every morning hoped that he would not be on the train. Never did I await the arrival of the mails with more anxiety and impatience.

One day, as Emma and I were returning from luncheon, the janitor of the building met us at the door. "A box came for you, sir, by express," he said. "I paid two dollars and twenty cents on it. It is up in your room."

I said nothing, but put my hand in my pocket. I began to count the money in my pocket-book, but my hand shook, and I dropped a quarter of a dollar on the floor, which rolled off to some distance. As the janitor went to pick it up, Emma approached me, and I noticed that she was very pale.

"If you haven't enough," she said, "I have some change with me."

I needed seventy cents to make up the sum, and Emma gave it to me. And then, without a word, we went upstairs. We did not hurry, but it was the first time, I think, that I ever became out of breath in going up those stairs. The moment we looked at the box we knew. The picture had been sent back.

I gazed at it blankly, reading over and over the painted address.

"Perhaps you had better open it," said Emma, in a very low voice. "It may not be——"

As quickly as I could I took off the centre board. The bull-calf, with a melancholy greeting in his eyes, looked out upon us. Then Emma sat down upon the nearest chair and burst into tears, and I drew near to comfort her.

Half an hour later I had taken the picture from the box, which I carefully searched. "Do you know," I cried, a sudden anger taking the place of the deadened sensation of my heart, "that this is an outrageous insult? He should have written to me before he sent it back; but to return it, without a word or line of any kind, is simply brutal."

I said a great deal more than this. I was very angry. I would write to Schemroth, and let him know what I thought of this. Emma now endeavoured to soothe my passion, and urged me not to do anything in a moment of excitement which might injure me in a business point of view. I did not promise forbearance, but suddenly exclaimed: "And then there is Osburn! He must be told. It will be a hard, hard thing to do! They will both be terribly disappointed. It will break up all their plans."

"I have thought about the Osburns," said Emma, coming close to me, and putting her hands upon my arm, "and I will tell you what we will do. I will go and see Mrs. Osburn. That will be much better than for you to see her husband. She will not be angry, and I can explain everything to her so that she will understand."

"No, my dear," said I; "that will not do. I shall not suffer you to bear what must be the very heaviest brunt of this trouble. In a case like this it is the duty of the man to put himself forward. I must go immediately and see Osburn at his office before he starts for home."

"I wish you would not," she said earnestly. "Of course the man ought to take the lead in most things, but there may be times when it will be easier and better for the wife to go first."

The moment she said these words she blushed, and I snatched her into my arms. The wife! If those rich lovers of art had only known what they might have made of this dear girl by buying my picture, it would never have come back to me.

But time was flying, and if I was to see Osburn at his office, I must hurry. The thing was hard enough to do, as it was, and I did not feel that I could have the heart to tell the story in the presence of his wife.

"If he is very much troubled," said Emma, "and says anything to you which you do not like, you will not let him make you angry, will you?"

"Oh no," said I; "I am not so unreasonable as that. I have so much pity for him that he may say to me what he pleases. I will bear it all."

"I am very sorry for you," said Emma, looking up at me, "and I do wish you would let me see Mrs. Osburn."

But I was firm in my resolution not to shift this very unpleasant duty upon Emma, and in a few minutes I had started down town. When I reached Mr. Osburn's place of business I found that he had gone home, although it was several hours earlier than his usual time of leaving. "He had something he wanted to attend to at his house," said one of the clerks.

This was a great disappointment to me, for now I would be obliged to go to see him that evening, and most probably to tell him the bad news in the presence of his wife. I did not fully appreciate until now how much easier it would have been to talk to him at his desk in the city. As I walked toward the Osburns' house just after dark that evening, I could scarcely believe that I was going to the place which I had lately visited with such delight. Emma and I had fallen into the way of already considering the house and grounds as our own, and as I opened the gate I remembered how we had stood there while I told her about some improvements I intended to make in said gate, so that the weight and chain would never fail to latch it. And now it made no difference to me whether the gate latched or not. And the flower borders, too, on each side of the path! How Emma had talked to me, when we had walked far enough away, so as to be sure not to hurt Mrs. Osburn's feelings, of what she intended to do in those borders! It all seemed to me like visiting the grave of a home. But I walked steadily up to the house. The parlour shutters were wide open, and the room was brightly lighted, so that I could see plainly what was passing within. There was an air of disorder about the pretty room. Mr. Osburn, in his shirt sleeves, was on a step-ladder taking down a picture from the wall, while his wife stood below ready to receive it. All the other pictures—the portraits of their parents and the chromos which Emma and I thought so little of, but which they valued so highly—had been already taken down. These, with various little articles of ornament and use, valuable to them on account of association with some dear friend or some dear time, were the things which they intended to reserve ; and it was plain that it was to take down and pack up these that Mr. Osburn had come home early that day. It was now only four days from the date he had fixed for surrendering the house to me, and he was working hard to have everything ready for us. He knew very well that Emma and I had arranged that we would be quietly married as soon as the house should be ours, and that in this charming home, all ready to our hands, we would immediately begin our married life. How earnestly and honestly they were doing their part !

I do not think I am a coward, but as I stood and gazed at these two I felt that it would be simply impossible for me to walk into that room and tell them that they might hang up their pictures again and un-pack their bric-à-brac, and that they were not going to take the pleasant journeys they had planned, until they had found some other person, more able to keep to his word than I was, who should take their house and buy their goods.

No, I could not do it. I would go home and write to Osburn. I did not feel that this was as manly a course as to speak to him face to face, but I could not speak to him now. As I was about to turn away, Osburn got down from the ladder, and they both looked around the room. Their faces wore an expression of pleasant satisfaction at the conclusion of their task, but mingled, I truly believe, with a feeling of regret that they should leave to us such bare walls. How Emma and I had talked of what we intended to do with those walls! How I had drawn little sketches of them, and how we had planned and arranged for every space!

I hurried home, wrote a note, and tore it up. I wrote another, but that too did not properly express the situation. It was late, and I could do no more. I would write in the morning, take the letter into town and show it to Emma, and then send it to Osburn at the office.

The next day Emma was in my studio reading the disgraceful confession I had written, when the janitor came in and handed me a letter.

"It is from Osburn," I exclaimed, glancing at the address, as the man closed the door behind him. "I know his handwriting. Now this is too bad. If Schemroth had only treated me with decent politeness I could have seen Osburn, or have written to him, before he felt himself obliged to remind me that the time had come for me to attend to my part of the contract."

"But you must not allow yourself to be so disturbed," said Emma. "You don't know what he has written."

"That is the only thing he could write about," said I bitterly, as I opened the letter. "It is very humiliating."

We read the note together. It was very brief, and ran thus :—

"DEAR SIR,—I have a customer who is willing to buy your picture, but he is dissatisfied with the foreground. If you will put in some daisies or other field flowers to brighten it up and throw the animal a little back, he will take it. I can ask him enough to cover your price and my commission. As I am sure you will make the alterations, I will forward the picture to you immediately.

"Yours truly,   L. SCHEMROTH."

The letter was dated four days previously.

We looked at each other, unable to speak. Our great cloud had turned completely over, and its lining dazzled us. We found words very soon, but I will not repeat them here. We could have fallen down and worshipped our painted calf.

"And now, my darling," I cried, "will you put the daisies in our picture?"

"Indeed will I," she said. And away she ran for her paints and brushes.

The rest of that afternoon she steadily painted, while I sat beside her, watching every touch of her brush.

"This daisy," she said, as she finished the first one, "is to make you happy, and the next one will be for myself; then I will paint two more for Mr. and Mrs. Osburn, and you must not fail to go and tell them to-night that you will settle up our business in a very short time; and I will paint a small daisy for Mr. Schemroth, and if he hadn't forgotten to mail his letter when it was written, I would have made his daisy bigger."

The picture soon went back to Boston, and the original of it now spends most of his time looking over the fence of his pasture into the pretty yard of the house where the Osburns used to live, and hoping that some one will come and give him some cabbage leaves. If he could see all that there is to be seen, he would see that the parlour of that house is hung with the spoils from the studios of two artists, that there is a room in the second story, with a northern light, in which flowers grow on canvas as beautifully as they grow in the fields and garden, and where a large picture is steadily progressing in which he figures as "The Coming Monarch." He would also see, far away on the Pacific shore, another couple whom he has helped to make happy; and if he could cast his eyes Bostonward he would see, every now and then, Mr. Schemroth writing to me to know when I could send him other animal pictures, and assuring me that he can find ready and profitable sale for all that I can paint. And, best of all, he could see, every day, Emma painting daisies into my life.

EVERY MAN HIS OWN LETTER-WRITER.

EVERY MAN HIS OWN LETTER-WRITER.

[MR. EDITOR,—I find, in looking over the various *Complete Letter-Writers*, where so many persons of limited opportunities find models for their epistolary correspondence, that there are many contingencies incident to our social and domestic life which have not been provided for in any of these books. I therefore send you a few models of letters suitable to various occasions, which I think may be found useful. I have endeavoured, as nearly as possible, to preserve the style and diction in use in the ordinary " Letter-Writers."

Yours, etc.,   F. R. S.]

No. 1.

From a little girl living with an unmarried aunt, to her mother, the Widow of a Unitarian clergyman, who is engaged as matron of an Institution for Deaf Mutes, in Wyoming Territory.

NEW BRUNSWICK, N.J., Aug. 12th, 1877.

REVERED PARENT,—As the morning sun rose, this day, upon the sixth anniversary, both of my birth and of my introduction to one who, though separated from me by vast and apparently limitless expanses of territory, is not only my maternal parent but my most trustworthy coadjutor in all points of duty, propriety, and social responsibility, I take this opportunity of assuring you of the tender and sympathetic affection I feel for you, and of the earnest solicitude with which I ever regard you. I take pleasure in communicating the intelligence of my admirable physical condition, and hoping that you will continue to preserve the highest degree of health compatible with your age and arduous duties, I am,

Your affectionate and dutiful daughter,
MARIA STANLEY.

No. 2.

From a young gentleman, who having injured the muscles of the back of his neck by striking them while swimming, on a pane of glass, shaken from the window of a fore-and-aft schooner by a severe collision with a wagon loaded with stone, which had been upset in a creek, in reply to a cousin by marriage who invites him to invest his

*savings in a patent machine for the disinte-
gration of mutton suet.*

BELLEVILLE HOSPITAL, CENTER CO., O.,
Jan. 12, 1877.

MY RESPECTED COUSIN,—The incoherency of your request with my condition [*here state the condition*] is so forcibly impressed upon my sentient faculties [*enumerate and define the faculties*], that I cannot refrain from endeavouring to avoid any hesitancy in making an effort to produce the same or a similar impression upon your perceptive capabilities. With kindest regards for the several members of your household [*indicate the members*], I am ever,

Your attached relative,
MARTIN JORDAN.

No. 3.

From a superintendent of an iron-foundry, to a lady who refused his hand in her youth, and who has since married an inspector of customs in one of the Southern States, requesting her, in case of her husband's decease, to give him permission to address her, with a view to a matrimonial alliance.

BRIER IRON MILLS, SECAUQUA, ILL., *July 7, '77.*

DEAR MADAM,—Although I am fully aware of the robust condition of your respected husband's health, and of your tender affection for him and your little ones, I am impelled by a sense of the propriety of providing in time for the casualties and fortuities of the future, to ask of you permission, in case of your (at present unexpected) widowhood, to renew the addresses which were broken off by your marriage to your present estimable consort.

An early answer will oblige,

Yours respectfully,

JOHN PICKETT.

No. 4.

From a cook-maid in the family of a dealer in silver-plated casters, to the principal of a boarding-school, enclosing the miniature of her suitor.

1317 EAST 17TH ST., N.Y., *July* 30, '77.

VENERATED MADAM,—The unintermittent interest you have perpetually indicated in the direction of my well-being stimulates me to announce my approaching conjugal association with a gentleman fully my peer in all that regards social position or mental aspiration, and, at the same time, to desire of you, in case of the abrupt dissolution of the connection between myself and my present employers, that you will permit me to perform, for a suitable remuneration, the lavatory processes necessary for the habiliments of your pupils.

Your respectful well-wisher,

SUSAN MAGUIRE.

No. 5.

From a father to his son at school, in answer to a letter asking for an increase of pocket-money.

MY DEAR JOSEPH,—Your letter asking for an augmentation of your pecuniary stipend has been received, together with a communication from your preceptor, relative to your demeanour at the seminary. Permit me to say, that should I ever again peruse an epistle similar to either of these, you may confidently anticipate, on your return to my domicile, an excoriation of the cuticle which will adhere to your memory for a term of years.

Your affectionate father,

HENRY BAILEY.

No. 6.

From the author of a treatise on molecular subdivision, who has been rejected by the daughter of a cascarilla bark refiner, whose uncle has recently been paid sixty-three dollars for repairing a culvert in Indianapolis, to the tailor of a converted Jew on the eastern shore of Maryland, who has requested the loan of a hypodermic syringe.

WEST ORANGE, *Jan.* 2, 1877.

DEAR SIR,—Were it not for unexpected obstacles, which have most unfortuitously arisen, to a connection which I hoped, at an early date, to announce, but which, now, may be considered, by the most sanguine observer, as highly improbable, I might have been able to obtain a pecuniary loan from a connection of the parties with whom I had hoped to be connected, which would have enabled me to redeem, from the hands of an hypothecater the instrument you desire, but which now is as unattainable to you as it is to

Yours most truly,

THOMAS FINLEY.

No. 7.

From an ambassador to Tunis, who has become deaf in his left ear, to the widow of a manufacturer of perforated under-clothing, whose second son has never been vaccinated.

TUNIS, AFRICA, *Aug.* 3, '77.

MOST HONOURED MADAM,—Permit me, I most earnestly implore of you, from the burning sands of this only too far distant foreign clime, to call to the notice of your reflective and judicial faculties the fact that there are actions which may be deferred until too recent a period.

With the earnest assurance of my most distinguished regard, I am, most honoured and exemplary madam, your obedient servant to command,

L. GRANVILLE TIBBS.

No. 8.

From a hog-and-cattle reporter on a morning paper, who has just had his hair cut by a barber whose father fell off a wire bridge in the early part of 1867, to a gardener, who has written to him that a tortoise-shell cat, belonging to the widow of a stage-manager, has dug up a bed of calceolarias, the seed of which had been sent him by the cashier of a monkey-wrench factory, which had been set on fire by a one-armed tramp, whose mother had been a sempstress in the family of a Hicksite Quaker.

NEW YORK, Jan. 2, '77.

DEAR SIR,—In an immense metropolis like this, where scenes of woe and sorrow meet my pitying eye at every glance, and where the living creatures, the observation and consideration of which give me the means of maintenance, are, always, if deemed in a proper physical condition, destined to an early grave, I can only afford a few minutes to condole with you on the loss you so feelingly announce. These minutes I now have given.

Very truly yours,
HENRY DAWSON.

No. 9.

From the wife of a farmer, who, having sewed rags enough to make a carpet, is in doubt whether to sell the rags, and with the money buy a mince-meat chopper and two cochin-china hens of an old lady, who, having been afflicted with varicose veins, has determined to send her nephew, who has been working for a pump-maker in the neighbouring village, but who comes home at night to sleep, to a school kept by a divinity student whose father has been educated by the clergyman who had married her father and mother, and to give up her little farm and go to East Durham, N. Y., to live with a cousin of her mother, named Amos Murdock, or to have the carpet made up by a weaver who had bought oats from her husband, for a horse which had been lent to. him for his keep— being a little tender in his fore-feet—by a city doctor, but who would still owe two or three dollars after the carpet was woven, and keep it until her daughter, who was married to a dealer in second-hand blowing-engines for agitating oil, should come to make her a visit, and then put it down in her second-story front chamber, with a small piece of another rag-carpet, which had been under a bed, and was not worn at all, in a recess which it would be a pity to cut a new carpet to fit, to an unmarried sister who keeps house for an importer of Limoges faïence.

GREENVILLE, *July* 20, '77.

DEAR MARIA, — Now that my winter labours, so unavoidably continued through the vernal season until now, are happily concluded, I cannot determine, by any mental process with which I am familiar, what final disposition of the proceeds of my toil would be most conducive to my general well-being. If, therefore, you will bend the energies of your intellect upon the solution of this problem, you will confer a most highly appreciated favour upon

Your perplexed sister,

AMANDA DANIELS.

THE END.

Edinburgh University Press:
T. AND A. CONSTABLE, PRINTERS TO HER MAJESTY.